Dylan Had Been Searching For Her For Eight Months, And Today He'd Hit Pay Dirt.

She didn't say anything, and neither did he. He kept staring at her, piercing her with his gaze. He thought she looked much too lean, as if she'd lost weight since the last time he'd seen her, as if she'd been to hell and back.

He knew she had.

"Julia," he finally said.

"My name is Janie Johnson," she replied, using her alias, pretending to be someone else.

Silence stretched between them, and Dylan cursed beneath his breath. Finding her had become his relentless pursuit. And now that he'd located her, she denied being Julia.

Her stubbornness struck a frustrated chord. She wasn't supposed to mess with his emotions. She wasn't supposed to twist him out of shape, to contort every gut-clenching part of his life.

But she did.

Dear Reader,

I decided to take this opportunity to talk about names, since the heroine in *The Morning-After Proposal* has three names: her real name, her alias and a nickname that more or less combines the two.

As for me, my birth certificate identifies me as Sheree (my dad had a thing for Sheree North, the blond fifties bombshell), and my pseudonym is Sheri. My mom calls me Sher (a childhood nickname), and my husband and most of my friends pronounce Sheree as Chérie—something I do, as well.

Every so often, a reader with the same name as one of my heroes or heroines contacts me. I've heard from several women named Kathy Lewis (she was the heroine in *Tycoon Warrior*). I also received an e-mail from a man named Skyler Hawk (he was the hero in *Skyler Hawk: Lone Brave*). The Skyler who wrote to me is from Hawaii, and his mother came across my book, bought a copy and gave it to him. She was surprised to see her son's name on a romance novel, and I was thrilled to hear from the "real" Skyler Hawk.

What's it like to name a character in a book? For me, it's a lot like naming a child, only with a wonderfully fictitious twist. Sometimes I talk to family members, asking for suggestions. Other times I consult baby books for first names, and when I'm stumped for last names, I page through the local phone directory or Native-American tribal registries, searching for a good fit.

And finally, to those of you about to embark on *The Morning-After Proposal* and read the final installment of THE TRUENO BRIDES trilogy, thank you, as always, for your support.

Love,

Sheri WhiteFeather

SHERI WHITEFEATHER

THE MORNING-AFTER PROPOSAL

Silhouette®

Desire

Published by Silhouette Books
America's Publisher of Contemporary Romance

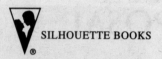

SILHOUETTE BOOKS

ISBN-13: 978-0-373-76756-4
ISBN-10:   0-373-76756-0

THE MORNING-AFTER PROPOSAL

This edition published by arrangement with Harlequin Books S.A.

® and TM are trademarks of Harlequin Books S.A., used under license. Trademarks indicated with ® are registered in the United States Patent and Trademark Office, the Canadian Trade Marks Office and in other countries.

Visit Silhouette Books at www.eHarlequin.com

Printed in U.S.A.

Recent Books by Sheri WhiteFeather

Silhouette Desire

The Heart of a Stranger #1527
Cherokee Stranger #1563
A Kept Woman #1575
Steamy Savannah Nights #1597
Betrayed Birthright #1663
Apache Nights #1678
*Expecting Thunder's Baby #1742
*Marriage of Revenge #1751
*The Morning After Proposal #1756

Silhouette Bombshell

Always Look Twice #27
Never Look Back #84

*The Trueno Brides

SHERI WHITEFEATHER

lives in a cowboy community in Central Valley, California. She loves being a writer and credits her husband, Dru, a tribally enrolled member of the Muscogee Creek Nation, for inspiring many of her stories.

Sheri and Dru have two beautiful grown children, a trio of cats and a Border collie/Queensland heeler that will jump straight into your arms.

Sheri's hobbies include decorating with antiques and shopping in thrift stores for jackets from the '60's and '70's, items that mark her interest in vintage Western wear and hippie fringe.

To contact Sheri, learn more about her books and see pictures of her family, visit her Web site at www.sheriwhitefeather.com.

To Diana Ventimiglia, my editor's assistant.
Sometimes Diana seems like my assistant, too.
She helped me with the production schedule on this
series, one hectic day after the other. Thanks, Diana.

One

Dylan Trueno had finally found her. And he wasn't letting her go.

Not this time.

Determined to make his point, he stared straight into her eyes, making her catch a stunned breath.

Instant recognition, he thought. The reoccurrence of a time-bomb attraction.

They stood face to face in the doorway of a cozy old house on the Rocking Horse Refuge. Dylan had been searching for her for eight months, and today he'd hit pay dirt.

He moved a little closer, and she took a step back. Just seconds ago, she'd answered the door to find him standing there, flinching at the sight of him.

She didn't say anything and neither did he. He kept staring at her, piercing her with his gaze. She wore a floral-printed blouse and slim-fitting jeans with a frayed hemline. Her face was devoid of makeup and her jewelry consisted of a simple gold cross.

He thought she looked much too lean, as if she'd lost weight since the last time he'd seen her, as if she'd been to hell and back.

But he knew she had.

Trapped, she glanced away and fidgeted with the ends of her hair. It was blonde now, but she was still the same girl who'd purposely disappeared.

"Julia," he finally said.

"My name is Janie Johnson," she replied, using her alias, pretending to be someone else. "But my boss calls me JJ."

Dylan assumed she worked for the old man who owned the refuge. "I spoke with Henry on the phone, and he's expecting me."

"He told me we were having company. A famous horse trainer. But I didn't even think—"

"That it would be me?" He wanted to reach out, to hold her, to lift her into his arms like he'd done before. But he kept his hands to himself. "This isn't a coincidence. I came here looking for you."

"You're mistaken. I'm not Julia."

"Yes, you are. We both know you are."

Silence stretched between them, and Dylan cursed beneath his breath. Finding her had become his relentless pursuit. And now that he'd located her, she denied being Julia.

Her stubbornness struck a frustrated chord. She wasn't supposed to mess with his emotions. She wasn't supposed to twist him out of shape, to contort every gut-clenching part of his life.

But she did.

Because he wanted her. He didn't care if they were practically strangers. That wasn't an issue for him. They'd shared a moment in time that went beyond logic.

The day they'd met, he thought. The day she'd cried in his arms. The day she'd almost kissed him.

"Why is Henry expecting you?" she asked suddenly.

"To discuss the fundraiser you're having."

"You lied to him? You offered to get involved?"

"I needed an excuse to look for you, to see if you were here. Would you have preferred that I told him the truth? Besides, you're lying to him, too." He challenged her, baiting her to admit who she was.

She did, in a disturbing way. "Henry knows me as JJ, and that's who I want to be."

"It's too late for that."

"Not if you go away." She fussed with her hair again, making the ends flutter, like wheat in the wind. "Not if you leave."

"I can't do that." He intended to take her home.

But first he had to tell her about her mother, to be the bearer of pain-packed news, something he would always despise himself for. "Come outside with me. I have to talk to you."

Just then, a graveled voice sounded in the background. "JJ, is that our guest?"

She paused, got a panicked look in her eyes. Like a doe caught in the sites of a rifle, she went anxiety-ridden still, imploring Dylan to protect her identity.

For now, he agreed. "We'll talk later." The last thing he wanted was for her to get the urge to bolt, to run away.

She nodded, and within seconds, Henry appeared. He was a kind, crusty cowboy, with a bent body and a craggy-lined face.

He greeted Dylan, shaking his hand a bit too vigorously. The old man seemed excited to meet him. Of course Dylan had acquired a level of fame. He traveled extensively in his line of work, and western riders from all over the country paid top dollar to attend his clinics and demonstrations.

Henry invited him inside, escorting him to a small, homespun parlor. Dylan took the chair closest to Julia and focused his attention on her, determined to stay by her side.

To not lose her again.

JJ's mind whirred like a tornado. Could she do this? Could she sit across from Dylan and pretend that he didn't affect her?

He looked exactly the way she remembered him. He was dressed in a denim jacket, Wrangler jeans and a silver-and-turquoise belt buckle that glimmered at his waist. He wore his rain-straight onyx-colored hair to his shoulders, and a western hat rested on his head.

A cowboy, she thought. An Indian. A man who'd invaded her dreams. A man she'd clung to a little too deeply.

He lifted the brim of his hat, revealing an even deeper, more intense expression.

A connection to Julia. To the woman she used to be.

"JJ is my Girl Friday," Henry said, interrupting her thoughts. "She's my part-time housekeeper, personal assistant and events planner. She helps with the horses, too."

"I'm impressed," Dylan responded.

"Thank you." JJ fought to keep her voice steady, to fake her way through this.

Dylan held her gaze, and the next bout of silence was deafening.

Like a chemistry project that was about to explode.

JJ released a shaky breath, and Henry became aware of the tension. He watched her and Dylan, closely, scooting to the edge of the sofa.

Not that Henry was clueless. He'd agreed to pay her wages in cash, suspecting that she was running from her past, even if he never probed her about it.

JJ wasn't the only drifter at the Rocking Horse Refuge. Henry didn't just take in abused and abandoned horses. He catered to troubled people, as well, letting his employees keep their secrets.

Until now.

Henry kept watching them, and JJ counted the seconds in her mind. One. Two. Three. Henry wouldn't remain quiet for long.

"What's going on?" he blurted. "Are you two sweet on each other? Did you know each other before?"

Dylan glanced at JJ, and her heart trembled. Henry thought she and Dylan were former lovers. That *he* was the reason she'd run away.

The famous horse trainer kept silent, neither affirming nor denying the romantic allegation.

Nervous, she turned to her boss. She wasn't about to admit that on the day Dylan had swept her into his arms, on the day he'd rescued her from a kidnapping, she'd almost kissed him, almost let the tenderness erupt into passion.

"This isn't what you think, Henry." She paused and chewed her bottom lip, tasting the waxy balm she wore.

"You sure about that?" he queried.

"Yes."

The old man frowned, furrowing his thin gray brows. He wasn't buying it. But neither was she. She remembered everything about Dylan: the breadth of his shoulders, the silkiness of his hair, the scent of hay and horses mingling with the faded note of his aftershave.

Dylan finally spoke. "It's time to talk," he told JJ. And to Henry, he added, "I'd like to be alone with her. It's important."

Her boss kept frowning. "I can see that it is."

JJ gave into the inevitable, agreeing to have a private conversation with Dylan. As she headed for the front door, Henry sent her a reassuring nod. He would be waiting.

Dylan followed her, and their footsteps echoed on wooden planks. The weather-beaten porch wrapped around the house like a rugged embrace. The Rocking Horse Refuge was located at the foot of a mountainous Nevada region, a place with grassy valleys and forested slopes. In the distance, the highest peak whitened the horizon with snow.

She glanced at the graveled driveway and foliage-draped yard. A snakelike chill coiled in the breeze, creating leaf-laden dust devils.

Dylan removed his jacket and handed it to her. "You forgot your coat."

She accepted his jacket, wishing that she didn't long to feel the roughhewn fabric against her skin, to inhale his scent.

"I've been searching for you since you ran away. My brother and my cousin are P.I.s, and I hired them to investigate your case and consult with the FBI. I know all about your phony ID." He watched her slip her arms into the denim sleeves. "But you don't have to keep hiding, to keep pretending to be JJ."

"Why? Because you found me?"

"Because the loan sharks who kidnapped you won't be able to hurt you again. They've been caught." His tone turned even more serious. "There was a hit man who was arrested, too."

Her knees nearly buckled. "What are you talking about? I was kidnapped to scare my mom into paying her gambling debt."

"I know. But after you and your mom took off, they put a contract on both of you."

Oh, God. She reached back, feeling for a chair, for a place to sit. Once she found it, she lowered herself onto the rickety wood. "Mom and I had a fight. We parted ways two months ago." She searched Dylan's gaze and saw an uneasy condolence in his eyes. "My mother is dead, isn't she?"

He sat next to her, taking an equally rickety chair. It creaked from his weight. "Yes, Miriam is gone. I'm so sorry, Julia."

Dizzy, confused, lost in sudden grief, she corrected him. "JJ. I'm still JJ."

"Not to me."

"I'm no one to you, Dylan. We met by accident."

His voice turned rough. "I buried your mother. I had a service for her."

Guilt assaulted her hard and fast, and she hugged his jacket, pulling it tighter around her body. "I shouldn't have argued with Mom. I shouldn't have left her." She rocked in her chair, feeling sick inside. "Was she shot? Is that how she died?"

"Yes."

The sickness remained. "Thank you for taking responsibility for her. You weren't obligated to do that."

"I convinced the FBI that I was. That Miriam needed me."

Because there was no one else, she thought. Besides JJ, her mother didn't have any family.

She didn't want to picture the woman who'd raised her being struck by a bullet, but the crimson-stained image presented itself, ripping into her mind, tearing at her conscience. "Where did you bury her?"

He shifted his feet, and his boots made a scraping sound. "Arizona."

"Where you live. Where I used to live." She caught a glimpse of untamed emotion in his eyes, and the look made him seem dangerous.

She didn't understand why he affected her that way. He'd done nothing wrong. On the contrary, he'd done everything right. He'd rescued her from a kidnapping; he'd given her wayward mother a resting place.

Then why did his soul seem so dark? Why did his eyes betray him?

"Come home with me, Julia."

"*JJ.*" Unable to control her reaction, she snapped at him.

"Julia." He snapped at her, too.

And then they stared at each other, a hard-edged, pulse-hammering, uncomfortably possessive moment passing between them.

This man, the handsome cowboy who'd done everything right, wanted to steal the identity she'd created. To force Julia to bury JJ—the way he'd buried her mother.

"Come home with me," he said again.

She shook her head, imagined herself in his arms. "No."

"You need to visit Miriam," he pressed. "To say goodbye to her."

Heaven help her. She didn't want to return to Arizona, to kneel beside Dylan at her mother's gravesite. To trace the headstone he'd chosen. To let him see her cry.

She'd already cried on the day he'd rescued her from the mess her mother had gotten her into. She'd already wept in his arms when he'd carried her out of that dirty, dingy trailer and into the desert sun.

How much more reliant on him could she be? And how much more pain could she bear from her mother's passing? From being safe at the Rocking Horse Refuge while her only parent lay dying?

"I loved my mom," she said. "But things were never right with us. Not even when I was a little girl."

"I know."

"Yes, of course you do." She frowned, realizing

she was still wrapped in his jacket, in the scratchy warmth he'd provided. "You hired P.I.s to investigate me. You uncovered my secrets."

"Maybe," he said. "Or maybe I just touched the surface."

No, she thought. He'd touched more than that. So much more. She removed his jacket and handed it to him. "I need to talk to Henry. To tell him what's going on."

"That's fine." The wind whipped Dylan's hair, blowing a loose strand across his face, creating a dark slash against granite-cut cheekbones. "But I'm not leaving this refuge without you."

When she walked to the front door and turned to look back at him, he looked directly at her, too.

Like a warrior who'd just raided a woman's heart.

JJ went inside and approached Henry. She knew the parlor, with its cherry wood curio cabinet and doily-covered end tables, was his favorite room in the house. But only because his wife had crocheted the doilies and had packed the curio with things that were special to her, including a faded photograph from their wedding day.

JJ glanced at the picture and tears sprung to her eyes. She didn't have any photographs of her mother. They'd run off in the middle of the night, leaving nearly everything behind. No keepsake items. No tangible memories.

"What happened?" Henry asked, when he saw her expression. "What did that boy say to you?"

"He told me that my mother was murdered." She gripped the edge of the sofa. "But he told me that he buried her, too."

Henry came forward and gave her a gruff yet tender hug. "I'm so sorry about your mama."

"Me, too." She knew the old cowboy understood grief. He'd been rattling around without his wife for the past five years. She gulped some air into her lungs and stepped back, afraid she would cry and not be able to stop. "I don't know what to say. How to explain all of this."

"Just start from the beginning, honey. Tell me who you are, and who Dylan is to you."

"My real name is Julia Joyce Alcott, and eight months ago Dylan rescued me from a kidnapping. He stumbled upon me by accident. Afterward, my mother and I left town, and Dylan started searching for us because he learned there was a hit man on our trail."

She kept talking, repeating everything Dylan had told her. Summoning personal details, she admitted that her mother was a compulsive gambler who'd borrowed an excessive amount of money from loan sharks and couldn't pay it back. "I didn't know who the kidnappers were until my mother told me what kind of trouble she was in. Then she begged me not to say anything. She said they would come after me again if we gave them up. But if we ran away, if we got new identities, we would be free. But once we were on the run, she started gambling again."

"So you and your mama had a falling out?" Henry asked, filling in the blanks.

"Yes. And that's how I ended up here and she ended up dead."

"That hit man could have gotten you, too." The old man shivered. "But you're safe now, JJ. And you'll always have a home here. You'll always be part of the refuge, even if we're struggling to make ends meet."

She glanced at a blue and white doily, where the pattern frilled into a scalloped edge. "Thank you, Henry."

They sat in silence for a moment. They both knew the refuge gave him purpose. He'd always been a cowboy, breeding cutting horses, but he'd started saving abused and abandoned animals after he'd lost his wife.

"So are you and Dylan sweet on each other?" he asked suddenly.

She shook her head, keeping her feelings, the heat Dylan evoked, to herself. "He keeps calling me Julia."

"'Cause that's the name he knows you by. Do you want me to call you Julia, too?"

"No. I want to be JJ."

"It still fits, you know. Didn't you say you're real name was Julia Joyce?" He sent her a small smile. "You can still be JJ."

She smiled, too. "Dylan wants me to go to Arizona with him to visit my mother's grave." Her smile fell. "But I don't know if I can."

"You have to, honey. You'll suffer inside if you don't make peace with her."

"But it's over now."

"No, it isn't. You haven't even begun to mourn. You're still in shock, still trying to wrap your mind around all of this. When it hits you, it's gonna tear you apart. And if you don't say a proper goodbye to your mama, it'll only get worse."

"Is that what happened to you when your wife died?"

He nodded. "I was angry at her passing on and leaving me alone. So for a while, I avoided saying goodbye. But that didn't do anything but mess me up even more."

JJ protested, defending her jumbled emotions. "I'm not angry at my mom for dying."

"No, but you're mad about the hell she put you through. And for that, you need to forgive her. So let Dylan take you back to Arizona to see her grave. Let him help you through this."

She fidgeted, folding her hands, unfolding them. "He told me that he wasn't leaving this place without me."

"He seems like a good one, honey. Someone you can count on."

Yes, she thought. But Dylan's valor didn't ease her

mind. Because she feared that by going home with
him, she was being kidnapped all over again.

And this time the man who'd rescued her, the man
who'd carried her to safety, was her captor.

Two

Dylan waited for Julia to return to the porch, frowning at the landscape, thinking about the uncharacteristic way in which she consumed him.

He'd never been a possessive man, not until he'd stumbled upon her, bound and gagged with barbed wire cuts stinging her skin. Not until he'd freed her from her bonds and she'd reached for him, needing him like no one had ever needed him before.

Dylan would always remember the way she'd grazed his cheek, the way she'd moved her mouth closer to his, the way she'd almost kissed him.

Soft, he thought. Sweetly sensual.

He refused to feel guilty for wanting her, for being

affected by her touch. He had something else to feel guilty about, something that was ripping a grenade-size hole in his chest.

Her mother's murder.

Dylan hadn't fired the gun, but he'd done something that had triggered the hit. He'd killed Miriam just the same.

But he couldn't tell Julia. Not now. Not this soon. The truth wouldn't bring Miriam back. It would only destroy what he intended to salvage with her daughter. The harshly tender, perilously intense connection.

He'd been living with the twisted need to protect Julia, to become part of her, even before her mother had died.

When the screen door creaked, his pulse jerked. Julia came outside and he stood up to look at her.

She inched forward. She'd put on a suede coat, but she still looked chilled.

And vulnerable.

The roots of her hair were coming in dark, defying the bleach she'd used. He knew she was an outdoorsy girl, but today she seemed lost, the power of the earth, of the trees, of the snow-capped mountains nearly swallowing her whole.

"Henry told me that I should go to Arizona with you," she said. "So I'm going."

Would he be able to purge his sin by taking Julia to her mother's grave? Would kneeing beside her in the aftermath of murder free him? "I'm glad Henry sees things my way."

"I have a feeling people always see things your way."

He frowned. "You don't."

"I never expected to run into you again. And certainly not like this." She slipped her hands into her pockets, burrowing into the lining of her coat.

He held her gaze. "So you tried to forget about me?"

"I tried to forget everything that happened."

"But you couldn't, could you, Julia?"

"No. Not completely. And please stop calling me that. I'm JJ, whether you like it or not."

He didn't like it, not one bit. She was pulling away from him already, not giving him a chance. "You're attracted to me," he said, refusing to let her deny the heat between them. "The way I'm into you."

Rattled, she glanced away, fighting whatever she was feeling. He could see the struggle.

"You saved me from a dangerous situation," she said, her voice cracking a little. "We both got caught up in that."

He had another theory. "If we'd met under different circumstances, we'd still be attracted to each other. It would still be there."

"Like some sort of cosmic energy?" She shook her head. "I don't believe in fate. I think people create their own destiny."

Dylan wanted to disagree, but he couldn't. He'd

gotten her mother killed. He'd created a tragedy that shouldn't have happened.

"We should try to get a plane out of here tomorrow," he said, changing the subject. "I'll book the flight."

She took a step back. "Why do we have to leave so soon?"

"What point is there in waiting? We both need to face this."

"Both?" She made a curious expression. "What do you need to face?"

He fought the guilt. "Nothing."

"Where am I supposed to stay when I'm in Arizona?" she asked.

"I have a guest room at my house. You can stay there."

She wet her lips, as though her mouth had gone dry. "I keep telling myself that I'm supposed to trust you. That there's nothing to worry about."

"I would never hurt you." He thought about Miriam's murder and felt his lungs constrict. "Not purposely."

"I know." She inhaled a deep breath, her chest rising and falling. Then she shivered, rubbing her arms, even though they were covered in suede. "You let me cry in your arms."

"We should go inside," he said, the twisted need to protect her coming back. "You should get warmed up."

She didn't respond. He didn't speak again, either.

He opened the screen door for her, and they entered the house.

Their silence bedeviling the air.

JJ fixed lunch. After being alone with Dylan, she needed something to do, something to keep her mind off of their intimate conversation.

While French onion soup simmered, she set the table, an old chrome and Formica booth that Henry and his wife had purchased from a bankrupt diner and reupholstered in a pretty fabric.

As she reached for the everyday china, white with tiny blue flowers, she thought about Henry's widow. Her name was Lois and her recipe box was still on the counter. JJ used it regularly. In some odd way she felt closer to Lois, a woman she'd never even met, than she did her own mother. The thought made her teary-eyed. At this point, she would do anything to have her mom back, to start their relationship over.

Finally the meal was ready. She told herself to relax and call the men for lunch. Dylan was still here, still making her nerves jangle. Henry was giving him a quick tour of the refuge, probably trying to convince him to get involved in the fundraiser.

She used a hand-held radio, a common communication system on ranches, to tell Henry to come inside and bring their guest.

When they arrived, Dylan smiled at her, a barely-there tilt of his lips, and her knees went girlishly weak.

"This looks good," he said.

"Thanks." She met his gaze, memories drifting in and out of her mind. His touch, his scent, the kiss that never happened.

After a beat of silence, Henry interrupted. "We can wash up at the sink."

By the time they sat down to eat, JJ couldn't think clearly. Dylan was beside her in the booth, his shoulder nearly brushing hers.

Henry devoured his soup, where thick slices of toasted bread and melted cheese had been placed on top. Dylan seemed to enjoy his, too. Along with the ham sandwiches and Caesar salad she'd prepared.

"Henry asked me to help with the fundraiser," Dylan said.

"We could use someone with his background," the older cowboy added.

She turned to her boss. "I knew you'd talk him into it."

"It didn't take much talking. He's happy to help. I told ya he was a good one."

"Yes, you did." She sent Henry a brave smile. She wasn't about to spoil this for him. If Dylan's participation in the fundraiser could keep the Rocking Horse afloat, then she who was she to complain?

"I owe this to Henry," Dylan said. "I misrepresented myself when I first arrived. You know, using the fundraiser as an excuse to see if you were here."

She speared a lettuce leaf. "Did you misrepresent yourself at other ranches, too?"

"Yes, but none of them are non-profit organizations. When I called them and set up phony meetings to discuss training their horses or conducting clinics or demonstrations, it wasn't for charity."

"How many other ranches did you search?" she asked, unable to quell her curiosity.

"I couldn't begin to count." He paused, studied her. "I've been all over this state. The FBI said you were probably hiding out on a horse farm in Nevada, working as a housekeeper."

"Because I used to be a maid at a motel?"

He nodded. "And because you like horses. They figured you'd be drawn to a ranch setting. They did a profile on you."

"Like on TV?" Henry seemed impressed. "I'm surprised they didn't flash JJ's picture on that missing person show."

She was glad they hadn't. She'd been bombarded with publicity right after the kidnapping, at least in her hometown. Dylan hadn't made the papers, though. He'd been reported as "the private citizen" who'd found her.

And now, eight months later, he'd found her again.

Like fate? Like destiny?

No, she thought. She'd already told Dylan that she

didn't believe in those things. She used to, when she was Julia. But JJ was trying to be stronger than Julia. She was trying to rule her own life.

Henry reached for his sandwich. "I figured you young folks could work together on the fundraiser."

Her pulse spiked. "Dylan and I?"

"Dylan has lots of rich acquaintances. The high-falutin horsey set who invite him to their parties and such."

JJ shook her head. "I don't see what that has to do with me."

Dylan spoke up. "I'd like you to attend some of those parties with me, to charm these people into making sizable donations or bidding on the horses you'll have up for adoption."

"It's a win-win situation," Henry put in. "Either way, The Rocking Horse comes out on top."

"It's a great idea." JJ's nerves cranked up a notch. "But I'm not really the party type. Dylan would probably fare better without me."

Henry disagreed. "Someone should be with him who represents the refuge. Besides, you've been cooped up here for months, hiding from the world. A couple of parties will do you good."

Would it?

She glanced at Henry and he smiled, boosting her confidence. He was right. JJ, the woman she was becoming, needed to break free, to live a less sheltered life.

"You better introduce me as JJ," she told Dylan.

He frowned a little. "What are you talking about?"

"At those parties."

He didn't respond, but she was glad she'd made her point. That she was fighting for her rights.

After the meal ended, Dylan returned to his motel room in town. But before he left, he asked JJ to walk him outside.

She got her coat, and they stood on the porch once again, with the breeze blowing bitterly around them.

"I'll call you later," he said. "To give you our flight itinerary."

"That's fine." She tried to keep their conversation light. "Henry seems thrilled that you're helping with the fundraiser and that I agreed to attend the parties."

"Maybe so. But I'm not introducing you as JJ."

She held her ground. "Yes, you are."

The wind kicked up a notch, rustling his jacket. "No, I'm not." He moved a little closer, scowled at her. "Being around you is so damn frustrating. Why can't you—" He stalled, traced the battered porch rail, running his hand back and forth, caressing the wood, nearly catching a splinter.

She sucked in a much-needed breath. "Why can't I what?"

"Behave like the girl I remember." He trapped her gaze. "The girl who almost kissed me."

Oh, God. Somewhere in the pit of her captive soul, she wanted to explore the knotted chemistry between them, to rekindle the moment their mouths had almost met.

But she wouldn't dare. Not while she was on the verge of going home with him.

Her voice betrayed her. "I'm not Julia anymore."

"Aren't you?"

She didn't reply, and he walked away without saying goodbye, without clearing the air. She watched him leave, wondering how long it would take for him to call.

After he was gone, she returned to the house, the forbidden kiss still lingering in her mind.

Hours passed, dragging with each tick of the clock. By the time the phone rang, JJ nearly jumped to answer it. Then she took a moment to calm her nerves. If it was Dylan, which she assumed it was, she didn't want him to know she'd been waiting for him.

She picked it up on the fourth ring. "Hello?"

"Julia?" It was him, being headstrong as ever.

Irritation hit her hard and quick. Waiting for his call had been a mistake. She decided not to respond.

"Julia?" he said again. "I know damn well you're there."

She glanced out her window and saw the wind snag a branch on a barren fruit tree. Two could play at his game. "Maybe I should start calling you Darrin or something."

He chuckled. "Like the husband in *Bewitched?* Are you trying to make a married man out of me?"

Heaven's no, she thought. He would make a lousy husband. He wouldn't even be able to get his wife's name right. "Okay. Fine. I'll call you Bob instead."

"I get it. Bob Dylan." This time he didn't chuckle. His voice was strong, silky, richly masculine. "I like his music. His lyrics." He paused, released an audible breath. "I've always been fascinated by the lady who is supposed to lay across his big brass bed."

Her pulse panicked, quickened, jumped to her throat. That song never failed to give her chills. Romantic, sexy, poetic chills. "Never mind. Call me Julia. Do whatever the hell you want." She frowned, considered hanging up on him. "You will anyway."

"You're right, I will." His tone didn't change; his voice remained strong and silky. "I have one, you know."

Dare she ask? "Have one what?"

"A big brass bed."

Sakes alive. JJ was in bed now, curled up in the predusk hours, wearing pink sweats and fuzzy socks. On the nightstand was a cup of herbal tea. Henry's dog, a sweet old bloodhound, napped beside her. "I'm not going to be her."

"Her who?" he asked, although she suspected that he knew.

"The lady in Dylan's big brass bed."

"Not his, no. But mine, yes. At least in my dreams. I already told you that I was into you, Julia."

She was into him too, but she shouldn't be. "You'll just have to keep dreaming."

"I've been doing that for eight months." He shifted or moved or did something that rustled the phone. "I haven't had a lover since then."

She went silent. Completely still. She didn't know what to say, how to feel, how to react.

"Did you hear me?" he asked.

"Yes." She regained her senses. Or she tried to. Her head was still reeling. "I'll bet that's a record for you."

He didn't comment on his record. Instead, he pried into her sex life. "Has it been a long time for you, too? Or is there someone I should be jealous of?"

She looked at the dog, then ruffled his ears. He opened his droopy eyes and yawned at her. "Craig is in bed with me now."

Dylan laughed. "I already met Henry's dog. That lazy old hound doesn't count."

She laughed, too. Then they both fell silent.

"It's going to happen," he said suddenly.

Her heart nearly blasted its way out of her chest. She knew he meant the kiss. "Not if I don't let it."

"You will. Sooner or later you will."

Struggling for control, she changed the subject. "So, what's the deal with our trip? Did you book the flight?"

He didn't respond. Instead he left her hanging, the intimacy he'd created hovering in the air.

She waited, her heart still pounding.

"Yes," he finally said. "I took care of it. We leave

tomorrow around three. I'll pick you up around eleven-thirty. That'll give us plenty of time to get to the airport and go through the security check and all that."

"I'll pay you back when I can," she said, grateful the tension had passed.

"What for?" he asked.

"The flight."

"I don't mind. I'd rather pay your way."

"I appreciate your generosity, but I don't want to be indebted to you. Not anymore than I already am." She could only imagine what her mother's burial had cost. But she would find a way to reimburse him for that, too. Even if it took years.

"I'll see you tomorrow, Dylan."

"Yeah. But I'll see you tonight, too," he said, ending the call as roughly as it had begun.

Stonewalled, JJ hugged the phone, the empty dial tone, to her chest. He'd done it again. He'd gotten in the last word, the last romantic thought.

He would see her tonight.

In the fantasy of his mind.

Three

At bedtime, Dylan went half-mad. He wasn't tired. Fresh from the shower, he was as wired as a tail-on-fire tomcat, stalking the motel room in his sweats.

He dragged a hand through his damp hair. Eight months, he thought. Eight-search-for-Julia months since he'd been with anyone.

He hadn't deliberately deprived himself. He'd gotten so caught up in her, so consumed in finding her that nothing else mattered.

And now he was suffering for it.

Dylan cursed, using the harshest word that came to mind. He hated feeling this way. If he could purge her from his blood, he would. He didn't like being enthralled by a woman. This wasn't his idea of fun.

And neither was taking her to the cemetery.

But he owed her that much. Hell, he owed her more than that. He owed her the truth.

So tell her, he thought. Tell her why the hit man was hired.

And risk losing her this soon? No way. No damn way. He needed more time.

He glanced at the clock and decided to call his cousin. Aaron could blow this for Dylan. Aaron knew too much. But so did everyone else who was involved in the case.

He cursed again, then took action, dialing Aaron's number. His cousin answered on the third ring.

"I found her," Dylan said, right after Aaron voiced the customary hello.

"Dylan?"

"Yeah, it's me."

"You found Julia?"

"Yes. She's at a horse refuge in Nevada. But she's coming home with me to see her mother's grave."

"Damn. You finally found her. Did you call the FBI?"

"No." He frowned at the phone. Here it comes.

"Why the hell not?"

"Because she isn't in danger anymore."

"They'll still need to talk to her. They'll want her to testify."

"I know." Dylan was testifying, too. "But I don't see the point in rushing things. They haven't even set a trial date."

"You just don't want Julia to hear all of the facts. But we keep telling you that what happened to Miriam wasn't your fault."

By "we" Aaron meant Dylan's family. But they were biased. They would never let him take the rap for his mistake. "Don't patronize me. Let me handle this on my own."

"And keep information from Julia? You're treading on dangerous ground."

"It's my ground. So stay off of it."

Aaron lit into him. "I always thought you were a jerk. Even when you were a kid."

"I'm not a kid anymore. And if I'm a jerk, so are you. You got married for revenge."

"I love my wife," came the defensive reply.

"And I want Julia. So if you ruin this for me, I'll beat you to a pulp."

"Screw you, Dylan."

"Yeah, whatever." He paused, stalked the room again, hit a snag with the cord and nearly dropped the phone.

"Promise me you'll call the feds," Aaron said. "Promise me you'll do the right thing."

"Fine. I'll call them." But he would do it on his own time, at his own pace. Not that he was going to admit that to Aaron.

"Good," his cousin said. "This isn't something to play around."

Dylan's heart tensed. "I wish I didn't want her."

"I guess it's too late for that. So when is she coming home with you?"

"Tomorrow," he responded, too damn anxious to see her again.

The moment JJ saw Dylan's ranch, the horse farm he owned, she struggled with her emotions. The kidnapping site was just miles away.

Was her mother's grave close by, too? Had Dylan chosen a resting place near his home?

If only her mom were still alive. If only they could work past the destruction.

Dylan turned toward her. "Are you okay?"

She feigned a positive response, wishing he wasn't so observant. When he glanced away, she looked out the window. The airport limo took them down a long paved driveway leading to a sprawling adobe structure where the desert swerved into what seemed like an endless expanse of acreage.

Dylan's success was showing. But so were his Native roots. Not that JJ knew anything about his culture. She didn't even know what tribe he was from.

The car stopped, and once they were standing on the pavement, Dylan took charge of their luggage and paid the driver.

Without speaking, Dylan escorted her inside. She

looked around the spacious living room and saw Old Mexico-style furniture, clay-tiled floors and roughly textured walls. Tiered windows curved in a sweeping line. A brick fireplace dominated the center of the room, with wooden crosses, Indian artifacts and brass relics on the mantle.

"Are we alone?" she asked.

"My ranch hands live out back."

"I was talking about a housekeeper."

He raised his eyebrows. "Do I look like I have a housekeeper?"

She couldn't help but smile. As beautifully primitive as his custom-built home was, it was ruggedly messy, too. Charmed with cowboy-type clutter. "No, I suppose not."

"Do you want the job?" he asked.

"You didn't bring me all this way to clean your house."

"No. But if I stole you away from Henry, you could be my mistress." When she widened her eyes, he added, "I don't see the problem with a woman being a housekeeper and a mistress. That's the kind of wife I want someday."

Stunned, she could only stare. What was he? A throwback from the fifties? A young, Stella-screaming Marlon Brando? "Please tell me you didn't really say that."

He shrugged, laughed. "You're so easy to tease, Julia. You fall for everything."

Because Julia was a fool, she thought. And JJ was learning to know better. "So what kind of wife *do* you want?"

"I'll take you," he said staring her down.

Her breath lodged in her throat.

"It was a joke," he said.

Was it? She couldn't tell. Either way, he'd just dropped a stick of dynamite onto her lap. As a little girl she'd secretly planned her wedding. She'd even dressed up in front of the mirror, holding a hand-picked bouquet of her favorite flowers.

Suddenly neither of them spoke. Not a word.

Finally, he defused the dynamite. "Do you want to see your room? Get settled?"

"Yes…please."

He picked up her bag and escorted her down the hall.

The guest room he offered was decorated with pine furniture and animal-skin accents. A calfskin throw was draped over the headboard of a queen-size bed.

"The bathroom is attached." He gestured. "Right through that door."

"Thank you. This is nice."

"I'm glad you think so." He moved closer and reached out to touch her hair, getting personal once again. "Are you going to dye it back to its natural color?"

"No. I'm going to keep being a blonde." Because Julia had dark hair, she thought. And JJ needed to be different from Julia.

He lifted her chin, looked into her eyes, spoke much too softly.

His voice all but caressed her. "You should stop fighting your identity. You are who you are."

The woman who still wanted to kiss him, she thought.

But worse yet was the child she used to be. The dreamy little girl standing in front of the mirror, dressed in white and waiting for Prince Charming to sweep her into his arms.

The way Dylan had done on the day he'd rescued her.

Before she leaned into him, before she lost what was left of her sanity, she panicked, clouding desire with death.

"We need to get ready to go to the cemetery," she said suddenly.

He started, frowned, stepped back. "We can't. It's too late. It'll be dark soon. We'll have to go tomorrow."

Trapped, confused, beguiled, she fussed with her suitcase, with the metal latch. Suddenly the airtight container seemed as constricting as a coffin. "Then I need to be alone."

His frown deepened, striking premature crow's feet near the corners his eyes. "For how long?"

Forever, she thought. But she told him to check on her in a few hours. After JJ had enough time to control Julia.

And convince her to stop wanting him.

* * *

Dylan came for her two hours later, but she'd expected as much. She was ready for him, or so she told herself.

But it was a lie.

"Do you want to have dinner on the patio?" he asked, standing in her doorway in a white T-shirt, slightly frayed jeans and the beautifully crafted belt buckle he favored. "I ordered takeout."

She accepted his invitation, assuming that his cupboards were bare. That his traditional adobe kitchen, with its copper pots and strings of dried chilies, wasn't stocked for guests.

JJ followed him outside. He hadn't done anything special to accommodate her. He'd simply placed the food cartons, the restaurant-style napkins and disposable drinks on a rugged wooden table and turned on the lights. But the scene was breathtaking. His flagstone patio flourished with greenery, with fragrant herbs and night-blooming plants.

"I have a gardener who takes care of all of this," he said.

"It's exquisite."

He smiled, laughed a little. "Exquisite? No one talks like that."

"I do." When she was overwhelmed, when something captivated her. "I love being outside."

"So do I. Sometimes when I can't sleep, I come out here, have a beer and watch the stars."

"I can hear the horses from here." The soft whinny of a broodmare, she thought. "That's nice, too."

"They make you feel alive, don't they? I specialize in AQHA, all-around and working cow horses."

"I'm glad you agreed to help with the fundraiser. Henry was right about your background. It should make a difference."

"Yeah. Malibu reeks of money."

"Malibu?" JJ went on alert. "As in California?"

"Didn't I mention that before?" He opened the food cartons and offered her a Mexican meal, sliding the combination platter in front of her, along with plastic utensils. "That's where my high-society clients live."

"The ones who have the parties? No, you didn't mention that."

"I guess I must have told Henry."

"But both of you neglected to tell me? Like a couple of good old boys who forgot about the female in the bunch."

He chuckled. "Good old boys? I'm only twenty-nine."

"Don't get smart. You know what I mean." She grabbed her drink, used the straw and sucked out a swig. She was only twenty-eight. "Someone should have told me. I thought the parties were here."

"In this modest little town?"

"Your ranch isn't modest."

"No, but it's not a mansion in Malibu, either. Wait

until you see those places. Houses as big as castles, stables that overlook the beach."

"The beach," she parroted.

"Yeah. You know…" He grinned, waggled his eyebrows. "The sand, the surf, muscle-bound guys, girls in itty-bitty bikinis."

"Knock it off." Now she was nervous about traveling to California with him, about jet setting to such a glamorous location.

He quit smiling, quit goofing around. "You'll do fine, Julia."

She scowled at him, hating that he'd tapped into her insecurities. "I'm not Julia," she shot back, wishing she hadn't given him permission to keep using her old name.

"You could have fooled me." He pointed to her food. "Now eat your dinner."

She glanced at the beef tamale, chile relleno and beans and rice he'd ordered for her. It was her favorite Mexican meal, her favorite combination platter. But he knew that, didn't he? He knew because it must have come up in his investigation. "Is this from Casa Maria?" she asked, referring to a local restaurant she used to frequent.

He nodded. "See? You're still Julia. You still like the same food, the same diet cola with extra ice, the same everything."

She wanted to throw her dinner at him, but she

was too darn hungry not to eat it. "Next time I want carne asada."

"Carne asada gives you indigestion."

"So do you." She plowed into the tamale, and he had the gall to laugh. She huffed out a breath. How annoying could he be?

"Did you know that my last name means thunder in Spanish?" he asked.

"Dylan Thunder?" She went after a scoop of rice.

"Dylan Curtis Thunder."

She liked his name, but she wasn't about to compliment him. "I guess I'd know that if *I'd* investigated *you.*"

He shook his head, indulged in his food. He was eating soft tacos and nachos on the side, with a slew of hot sauce.

Enough to make her mouth burn without even tasting it.

"You need to calm down," he said. "To relax."

"And you need to stop telling me what to do. To stop being so aggressive."

"I can't change who I am anymore than you can."

"You can try," she argued.

"But I don't want to." He smiled, cracked a joke. "It's the warrior in me."

She decided that he wasn't far off the mark. "What tribe are you from?" she asked, unable to curb her curiosity.

"White Mountain Apache." He sat back in his

seat, the amber glow from the outdoor lighting casting a soft, shadowy ambience. "My parents are originally from the rez, and I'm a full blood, but I wasn't raised in an overly traditional way."

To her, he seemed rooted to his heritage. She'd seen signs of it all over his house. On his person, too. "So do your brother and cousin live close by?" JJ recalled that that they'd been involved in her case.

"They live in L.A. You can meet them when we go to California. Oh, wait. You already know my brother's fiancé."

She started. "I do?"

He nodded. "Carrie Lipton. Her parents own the motel where you used to work."

"Carrie? She was divorced when I knew her, from a man named—"

"Thunder," Dylan supplied, laughing a little. "That's what everyone calls my brother. They were married when they were teenagers, divorced for twenty years, and now they're engaged again."

"Wow." She hadn't made the connection. "What about your parents? Where do they live?"

"About ten miles from here. You can meet them, too." He sat forward again, shifting in his chair. "Everyone in my family has been worried about you."

Suddenly she wanted to curl up and cry in his arms, to mourn her mistakes. "I miss my mom."

"I'm sorry, Julia. So incredibly sorry."

"Thank you." At that moment, she *was* Julia. The woman who'd lost someone she'd loved.

She met Dylan's gaze and saw a dark cloud in his eyes. There were so many things he hadn't said. So many details about her mom they hadn't discussed. But she couldn't bring herself to bombard him with questions, to absorb the tragic answers in her grief-stricken mind. Not now. Not tonight.

She took another bite of her food and felt the comfort in it: the south-of-the border flavor, the familiar spices. Sometimes she used to eat at Casa Maria with her mother.

"Are you going to be all right tomorrow?" he asked.

She knew he was talking about visiting the cemetery. "I'll be fine," she said, praying that saying goodbye to a headstone would be enough. "Can we stop and get some roses first? Mom liked roses."

"Of course we can." He quit eating. "What's your favorite flower?"

The little girl in the mirror came back, and she fought a wave of romance, of white lace and make-believe promises. "You mean you don't know? It isn't typed in a report somewhere?"

"No, it isn't." He reached across the table to touch her hand. "But if you tell me, I'll buy you a zillion of them."

"Then I'm not telling you." Not at the expense of

the sad and lonely child she used to be. "I won't let you court me."

"It's too late," he told her, his fingers igniting hers. "I already am."

Four

In the morning Julia entered the living room, dressed and ready, clutching a leather purse and lightweight shawl.

Dylan was ready, too. He sat on the couch, drinking coffee. He'd been waiting for her.

"Hey." He stood and lifted his cup. "Do you want some? I made a fresh pot."

"No, thank you." She put her hand on her stomach, and he suspected she was too nervous to handle a burning boost of caffeine.

"What about breakfast?" he asked, wondering if a meal would settle her system. "We could do something simple. Maybe some fast food."

She shook her head. "I'd rather eat later if that's okay with you."

"No problem." He was uncomfortable about going to the cemetery, too. But he wasn't about to let it show.

Julia fussed with her clothes, and he noticed the detail on her blouse. A row of rhinestone buttons embellished the feminine fabric, and he wondered if she'd worn something pretty for her mother.

"Did you sleep all right?" he asked.

She quit fussing. "I tried to get some rest, but I kept tossing and turning."

He'd been up half the night, too. "We should go." Get this over with, he thought. Deal with the consequences.

She agreed, and they left the house and climbed into his truck. He drove to a nearby florist, and she roamed the shop.

Dylan didn't interfere. He stood back, watching her, respecting her space, the chilled air around her. Although the environment was bright and colorful, rows of glass-front refrigerators made it seem cold, morguelike.

Or maybe it was the memory of viewing her mother's lifeless body. Of knowing the bullet hole had been patched up and smoothed out with mortician's wax.

Julia chose a bouquet of pink roses, and he moved forward to pay for them. She tried to stop him from footing the bill, but Dylan handed the sales clerk his credit card anyway.

"I'm keeping tabs of how much I owe you," she said, after they left the store, the flowers pressed protectively against her chest.

"Men are supposed to pay," he told her, as they got back on the road.

"This isn't a date. We're going to my mother's grave."

He frowned, stopped at a red light, hit the breaks a little too hard. "I didn't mean it like that."

"I know. I'm sorry. It's just that you've done so much already."

Yeah, he thought, he'd done plenty. He'd gotten Miriam killed.

By the time he entered the gates of the cemetery, he felt trapped. The sky was a picture-perfect shade of blue, and junipers dotted the softly rolling terrain.

But death was all around them.

He took a winding path to the top of a grassy slope, and when he parked his truck, she released a quaking breath.

Without speaking, he led the way. Markers of all shapes and sizes offered names, dates and loving memories.

Finally Dylan stopped at Miriam's headstone.

"It's pink." Julia's voice broke. "Like the roses." She knelt to the ground, putting the flowers in place, arranging them just so. "But you knew, didn't you? You knew pink was her favorite color."

He knelt beside her and squinted into the sun. Spring danced dramatically in the air, making leaves sway and grass shimmer. "I didn't know for sure. But her room at your apartment had lots of pink in it."

"You were at our apartment? When?"

"A few weeks after you and Miriam disappeared. By that time, the FBI had already ruled it out as a crime scene, so I convinced your landlord to let me look around."

She touched the pastel marker, tracing Miriam's name, using the tips of her fingers. "What happened to the things we left behind? Do you have any of it?"

"No." He watched a strand of her hair blow across her cheek. "I assumed your landlord was going to put everything in storage, but he got rid of it. I would have stopped him if I'd known."

"How closely did you look around?" She sat back on her heels, tried not to teeter. "Did you page through our old photos? Did you see pictures of me when I little?"

"Yes." He'd been captivated by her photographs, by her innocence. Julia had been a sweet, knobby-kneed child with dreamy eyes, spidery lashes and scattered freckles. "I saw pictures of your dad, too."

"He died when I was a baby. Before Mom and I moved to Arizona. But we were always moving."

Dylan nodded. He was aware of every town, every

city, every place she'd ever lived. In the past eight months, he'd been to all of them.

She focused on the roses. "Mom was forever in trouble, running away from her debts, from past-due rents and phone lines that were being disconnected. She tried to make it seem like an adventure, like we were gypsies or something. But I sensed that something was wrong, even then."

He turned to look at the headstone. "But not this wrong."

"No. I never thought it would end like this. I'm an adult, but I feel orphaned." She reached for her shawl and slipped it over her shoulders, hugging herself with the loosely woven knit.

Shallow comfort, he thought. "You should have called."

She blinked. "What?"

"After I rescued you that day, after everything was over. I gave you my number. I told you to call me if you needed anything. But you ran away instead."

"I didn't want to drag you into my life any deeper than you already were. I was already scared of—"

"The way I made you feel?" He raised his voice a little, then caught himself and lowered it, afraid of waking the dead, afraid of being found out.

"I don't want to talk about this." She tightened the shawl, her downcast eyes edged with tears. "Not here."

Hell and damnation. What was he doing? Punishing her for the secret he was keeping? "I'm trying to do right by you. I swear I am."

"I know." She picked at a blade of grass. "You wouldn't have buried my mother if you weren't." Finally she looked up, heightening his guilt. "Will you tell me about her service?"

The air in his lungs went tight. "There isn't much to tell. It was small, simple. Just my parents and me." He glanced at the sky, wondered if Miriam was listening and if she knew how sorry he was. "We did our best to honor her. We sprinkled ashes and pollen around her grave before her casket was lowered. To ensure that her soul would go to heaven."

Julia swiped at her watery eyes, making him want to touch her, to hold her, to pull himself into mindless oblivion. And forget that he was responsible for her pain.

"Is that what the Apache do for their loved ones?" she asked.

"It depends on the family, on their traditions. My parents don't normally follow the old ways, but they do when someone dies," he added, unable to purge his sin, to stop it from clouding his mind.

After they left her mother's grave, JJ gazed out the window. The grassy slopes of the cemetery were gone, but the ache inside her wouldn't go away.

"Do you think your parents are home?" she asked.

"Why?" Dylan turned, searched her gaze, kept his voice quiet. "Do you want to stop by their house?"

"Could we? You said I could meet them. And after everything you told me, I'd really like to get to know them."

He nodded and made a U-turn, and soon they were headed down a long, empty highway.

Twenty minutes later he stopped at an ancient house with trees that had grown twenty to thirty feet tall, and JJ felt a sudden sense of peace.

She noticed gingham curtains in the windows. "Is this where you grew up?"

He parked in the graveled driveway. "Hellion that I was."

Curious, she studied him. His licorice black hair was plaited into a single braid, and his jaw was cleanly shaven. "You used to get into trouble?"

"I'm not as good as Henry thinks I am."

Her pulse fluttered, beating softly at her neck. "Maybe his idea of good is different from yours."

"Maybe." He unlocked her door, and the automatic latch clicked. "Ready?"

She got out of the truck, trying to picture him as a youth, as a wild-spirited boy. But all she saw was a tall, dark, strongly possessive man.

He entered his parents' house without knocking, took JJ's hand and led her through the ranch-style structure. He found his mother drying herbs in the kitchen. She wore earth-toned clothes, and her gray-streaked hair was coiled in a loose bun and clipped with a tortoise-shell ornament.

She glanced up, took one look at JJ and gasped. "Oh, my goodness. You're Julia, aren't you?"

"Yes." JJ wanted to embrace her, but she stood awkwardly instead, feeling orphaned once again. "But I prefer to be called JJ."

"Then JJ it is." Dylan's mother, who introduced herself as Margaret, came forward and initiated the hug. "It's so good to see you. To know you're safe."

"Thank you." She put her head on Margaret's shoulder, and the tears she'd fought at the cemetery streamed down her cheeks.

"Oh, honey. Oh." The older woman rocked her. "You'll be okay. We'll make it okay. Won't we, Dylan?"

JJ looked up and saw him frown.

"We can't bring Miriam back, Mom."

"No, of course not. But we can comfort JJ. We can treat her right."

"I'm trying," he said.

"Yes, he is," JJ agreed, troubled by his expression, by the darkness she often saw in his eyes.

He frowned again, then handed her a napkin to dry her tears. The quiet act of comfort almost made her cry even more.

Concerned about making a spectacle of herself, JJ stepped back and felt the walls closing in.

Margaret came to the rescue, suggesting that Dylan take her outside. "Why don't I make some iced tea while you show JJ around. You can look for your dad, too. I think he's in the barn."

Grateful for the reprieve, JJ followed Dylan willingly, anxious to take a much-needed breath, to inhale the pinion-laced air.

As they headed toward the back of the property, she tried to make easy conversation. The tear-dampened napkin was still clutched in her hand.

"Your family has a lovely home," she said.

"Carrie and Thunder got married here." He indicated a rustic gazebo and the ivy twining in circles around it. "I remember how pretty I thought Carrie was. Dressed in white and all that."

She shoved the napkin in her pocket, felt it crumple in the tight space. "How old were you?"

"Nine."

"And you had a crush on the bride." A sweet, syrupy warmth juiced her veins, and she tried to will it away. JJ was around nine when she'd secretly planned her wedding.

"I got over it." Long and lean and cut with rangy muscles, he squared his shoulders. "Boys don't have crushes for very long."

Girls do, she thought. But she didn't say so out loud.

They walked side by side, taking a path lined with spiny shrubs. The weathered barn came into view, and she realized the Truenos had chosen a simpler life than their famous horse-trainer, society-socializing son.

"What do your parents do?" she asked.

"Do? You mean for work?" His boots crushed a scatter of mulchlike bark. "They're both retired now, but Mom used to sell her jewelry at powwows, and Dad was a conservation biologist."

She couldn't help but be impressed. "She's a craftswoman, and he helped save the earth. I would have loved to have parents like that."

"They're good people. I always knew they were, but that didn't stop me from rebelling, from breaking the rules."

"Are you still breaking them, Dylan?"

"I am with you." He turned toward her, making the path seem narrower. Then his voice went hard, ruggedly heated, like the sun that chopped between them. "I don't like getting worked up over a woman."

Uncomfortable, she tried to get away, to create a wider berth, but a prickly plant snagged the side of her blouse, clawing the corner of her sleeve. "I didn't do anything to work you up. I—"

He just looked at her. One intense look, and she knew she'd said the wrong thing.

He moved closer. Close enough to weaken her knees. To leave her on the verge of what came next.

JJ panicked, afraid that he was going to kiss her.

But he didn't.

Instead he leaned forward and brushed his lips past hers, nearly touching, nearly making contact, the way she'd done to him on the day he'd rescued her.

"You know what you did," he said, on the beat of a whisper. "You know."

She stepped back and almost stumbled. But he didn't catch her. He let her regain her own footing.

Neither of them spoke. The foliage-draped path cast shadows across his face, across his granitelike features.

She felt as if she were trapped in a maze with no way out. Yet the barn was only a few hundred feet away.

Dylan's dad walked out of the weathered building, and JJ released a struggling-to-stay-calm breath.

The older man met them halfway and introductions were made. His name was Nolan, and he stood tall and solid, as grounded as the trees that graced his property. When he smiled, lines crinkled at the corners of his eyes.

She returned his smile, then fell into step with Dylan, his nearness making her much too aware.

Of wanting him. Of needing him. Of being at his mercy.

They joined Margaret on the patio where she had a pitcher of iced tea waiting, where JJ accepted the heartfelt hospitality the Truenos provided.

And wished she wasn't falling for their son.

JJ couldn't sleep. At four in the morning she climbed out of bed, slipped on her robe and exited her room. Then she glanced down the hall and noticed that Dylan's door was open.

He was up, too?

Curious, she crept closer, poked her head in the doorway and caught sight of the brass bed he'd told her about. Only it was unmade, tousled with sheets, pillows and a Pendleton blanket.

She wanted to step farther into his room, to riffle through his belongings, the way he'd gone through everything at her apartment. But she didn't have the courage to open dresser drawers, to pick up the book he'd left on the nightstand, to see what dates, if any, he'd marked on the calendar beside his computer.

So she remained where she was, scanning the masculine clutter from a safe distance.

He'd left the adjoining door to his bathroom open, and she could see his shower enclosure and the towel he'd draped over it. His toothbrush was on the counter, along with a black comb, a handful of ponytail holders and a bottle of cologne. She couldn't tell what brand it was, but she knew how inviting it smelled. He wore the same fragrance every day.

"Are you looking for me?" a deep voice said from behind her.

Dylan.

She winced, spun around, wished she'd had the good sense to stay away.

There he stood, with no shoes, no shirt and a pair of barely zipped jeans.

"I noticed you were awake," she said. "And I wondered where you were."

"I was outside. Having a beer."

"Oh, right. You do that when you can't sleep." She tugged at her robe, closing it a bit more.

He shifted his feet. "As long as we're both up, do you want hang out with me?"

Yes, she thought. She wanted to invade his privacy the way he'd invaded hers. "In your room? What for?"

"To the kill the insomnia, I guess."

"Okay." She took a chance and inched forward. One baby step, she thought. Like Mother May I. Like the game she'd played as a child. She wondered if her mom would appreciate the sentiment.

"I'm not going to attack you, Julia."

Feeling foolish, she took a couple of bigger steps. "You almost kissed me today."

"Turnabout is fair play. And I'm not masochistic enough to *almost* kiss you here. Besides, when I do it again, it'll be the real thing."

She wasn't about to ask when or where he intended to make good on his claim.

He sat at his computer desk chair, leaving the big brass bed for her. She perched on the edge of it and told herself this wasn't as intimate as it seemed.

But she knew better.

And so did he.

"This was a bad idea," she said.

"Not if you show me what you have on under your robe."

She stared at him.

His lips curved, ghosted, teased. "I was kidding, Julia."

"You and your sense of humor." Refusing to be outdone, she opened the terrycloth cover, flashing a pair of prim white pajamas. The trashiest lingerie she owned.

He raised his eyebrows, and they both laughed.

She decided to come clean. "Do you know why I was poking around your room? To snoop," she told him, answering her own question. "To find out the kind of information about you that you know about me."

"Really? That'd be fine if these walls could talk, but they can't."

"I wasn't looking for sexual secrets."

"I know some of yours."

Her jaw all but dropped. "Like what?"

"Like who your first lover was and where you lost your virginity."

Mortified, she threw one of his pillows at him.

"Dan Myers," he said. "It happened after the senior prom. You were wearing a red dress with a carnation corsage. Carnations aren't your favorite flower, are they?"

"No. And Dan told you all of that?"

"He told my brother. Thunder interviewed him. But that was about as detailed as it got."

"That's detailed enough."

He threw the pillow back at her. "If Dan wasn't married now with a couple of kids, I'd kick his ass."

"He broke up with me after we graduated. I was devastated."

"I'm aware that he hurt you." He looked straight at her. "I wish I would have known you then. That we would have gone to the same school."

Her heart went haywire. "So you could have been my first?"

"So I'd know what your favorite flower is."

Caught off guard, she wondered how a man could be so sweet, so sexual, so confusing.

"Who was your first?" she managed to ask.

"I don't remember her name. We met at the river, had a one-day tryst and never saw each other again."

"Sounds like a teenage boy's dream."

He swiveled in his chair. "It was."

She clutched the keep-away pillow. "I bet she remembers your name. I'll bet she remembers everything about you."

He merely shrugged.

"What about later?" she asked. "Has there been anyone significant?"

"I've slept with a lot of women. Notches in the bedpost and all that."

"Yes, of course." She could have kicked him for his cavalier response. His metal bedpost was as shiny, as unmarked, as a newly minted coin.

He changed the subject. "We should leave for California soon."

She waited a beat. "How soon?"

"Tomorrow. The next day. As soon as you're ready to meet the rest of my family. And hit those revolving parties."

"Don't we need to be invited?"

"I'm always invited."

"Why?" Envy reared its ugly head. "Because that social scene used to be part of your dating pool?"

He tensed, gave her a frustrated look. "Does it matter?"

"No," she said, doing her darnedest not to care. "We can leave for California any time. Any time at all."

Five

Dylan wanted to make the best of their trip, so he chose a hotel that offered private bungalows and lots of atmosphere. Nestled in the heart of the city, it provided a touch of Old Hollywood, with elegant furniture and black-and-white artwork on the walls.

"This is beautiful," Julia said, even though she frowned.

"I'm glad you like it." He frowned, too. Their place came with a cozy kitchen, a garden-style courtyard and two master suites. "You can take the girly room."

"The one with the sunken tub? I shouldn't have let you splurge like this."

"If you start in about owing me money, I'll clobber you." He wasn't about to admit that he'd picked a bungalow-style hotel so they could share the same accommodations. "By the way, I invited Thunder and Carrie to stop by and see you. And Aaron and Talia, too." He paused, explained further. "Aaron is the cousin I told you about, and Talia is his wife. They went undercover to search for you and your mom, to try to shake up the investigation."

She sat on the sofa. "Because you hired them to look for us?"

He nodded. "Aaron posed as a gambler so they could check out Gambler's Anonymous."

"My mother never went to any meetings."

"I know." He opened the drapes and watched the light spill over her, the sun catching the paleness of her hair. "But you did."

"Just once." She glanced out the window, her words tinged with softness, with sadness, with the kind of melancholy associated with death. "After Mom and I argued. After she stormed off and I never saw her again."

The beginning of the end, Dylan thought.

He poured two sodas from the bar, sat next to her and handed her a diet cola. When she took the drink, their fingers brushed.

In the tingling silence, he studied her. She still had a scatter of freckles. They were lighter, less pronounced than when she was a kid, but he could see them.

"I just wanted you to know how wrapped up Aaron and Talia were in your case," he said.

"Did they catch the hit man?"

He shook away a chill and hoped it wasn't Miriam's ghost. "No, the FBI did. But Talia and Aaron told me about your mother's murder." And he recalled how carefully he'd controlled his emotions, not wanting to break down in front of his cousin.

"Are you still in touch with the FBI?"

He nodded.

"So they know that you found me? That I'm in California with you?"

His heart hit his chest. He hadn't told the feds that he'd located Julia. He was still buying time, still preserving his secret.

"Yes," he told her, flat-out lying. "They know."

She folded her hands on her lap. "I guess I'll hear from them after we get back. I assume they'll want me to testify."

"The trial is a ways off." For which he was grateful. If Julia talked to the feds too soon, he would lose her for sure. He had to strengthen their bond. He had to win her over first. "Don't worry about the FBI. There's plenty of time for that. You have other things going on right now."

"Like the fundraiser?" She managed a smile. "And attending those soirees?"

"Exactly." He glanced at a nearby painting where the long lithe figure of a 1930s starlet made a glamorous statement. "I'm going to take you shopping. The first party is black tie and the second one—"

She cut him off. Her smile was gone. "You're not spending another dime on me."

"Do you have anything to wear?" he fired back, frustrated with himself, with her, with nothing being easy.

"I wasn't planning on going naked."

"You know what I mean."

"I brought a basic black dress with me."

"For two parties?"

"I'll wear different accessories."

He pointed to the painting. "You should get fixed up like that."

"And you should stop trying to turn me into the socialites you used to date."

Was she kidding? That was the last thing he was trying to do. The *very* last. Dylan had spent a lifetime trivializing his first "socialite" affair and making high-society sex insignificant.

A knock sounded on the door, and he cursed. He didn't give a damn what she said. He was choosing her wardrobe, buying whatever the hell he wanted.

He flung open the door and saw Aaron and Talia.

Aaron looked like the successful security specialist he was, attired in dark clothes and designer sunglasses. Beside him, Talia wore a slim-fitting pantsuit. A ruby and diamond wedding ring glittered on her finger.

The happy couple.

Aaron lowered his sunglasses. "What's wrong?"

Dylan stepped back. "Everything."

They entered the bungalow and everyone stood a little awkwardly. Dylan knew he should introduce Julia, but he didn't. He shot her an annoyed look instead.

Talia swept past him. Slim and chic with stiletto heels and bombshell-blonde hair, she headed straight for Julia. "Did he do something to upset you?" She turned toward Dylan. "Did you?"

He didn't respond, and Talia narrowed her gaze. "You went crazy searching for this girl and now you're being a jerk?"

He rounded on her. "Who said I was being a jerk?"

"Me," Talia snapped. "And here I thought you were different from Aaron and Thunder." She softened her voice. "More romantic."

Dylan didn't know what to say. So he glanced at Aaron, who gave him an irritated look. Great. Now his cousin was ticked. Apparently Aaron didn't appreciate the comparison.

Julia finally spoke up, telling her side of the story. She even used the "JJ" card, claiming that Dylan was trying to mess with her identity.

Talia, with her femme fatale attitude and overly independent nature, sided with Julia and an instant bond was formed.

They chatted like magpies, with Talia praising

Julia for sticking to her guns. "With the right hair and makeup your dress will be fine."

"Will you help me get ready when the time comes?" Julia asked.

"Of course I will." Talia snubbed her nose at Dylan. "Then you don't have to be obligated to him."

Like hell, he thought.

Luckily his cousin agreed. Aaron didn't seem annoyed anymore, at least not at Dylan. At this point, it was a matter of pride.

Male principle.

He leaned into Dylan, keeping his voice low. "You should buy her something anyway."

"I intend to. Dresses, shoes, purses, jewelry. The whole shebang."

"Sounds good to me."

"Yeah, well, your wife better not talk her out of wearing them."

"Are you kidding? Miss Clotheshorse? She'll take one look at everything and want it for herself. By the time this is over, I'll have to buy *her* something."

A few minutes later Thunder and Carrie arrived, and Carrie and Julia got reacquainted.

When Thunder joined the men, it didn't take him long to sense that something was going on.

So Dylan filled him in, explaining that he had less than forty-eight hours to secretly shop for Julia.

Making him wonder just how stupidly romantic he was.

On Friday Talia and Carrie came over to help JJ get ready for the first party. The second glamour-and-glitz gala was the following night, but she couldn't think beyond her crackling nerves, beyond getting through one high-society event at a time.

Dylan was nowhere to be seen. He'd left the bungalow hours ago, leaving her alone with the other women, as well as the hotel maid, who was vacuuming down the hall.

But it didn't matter. Because JJ had won the battle. She would be wearing her own dress.

"I can't tell you how much I appreciate this." She gazed at the transformation in the mirror. "It makes me feel like one of you."

"Because you are." Talia stood behind her at the bathroom vanity, twisting her hair into a loose chignon, with newly highlighted pieces framing her face.

"You became one of us the moment you met Dylan," Carrie said. "Once you get close to a Trueno man, there's no turning back."

Talia laughed. "She should know. She's marrying the same big lug again."

Carrie laughed, too. She had reddish-brown hair, tanned skin and radiant glow. She was pregnant with Thunder's child. "He isn't a lug."

"Sure he is." Aaron's wife added another bobby pin to JJ's chignon. "They all are. But they're irresistible, too."

JJ felt marginally better. The other women understood her need for independence. But they understood her attraction to Dylan even more.

The heat. The danger.

"Has Dylan kissed you yet?" Talia asked.

Her heart went batty. "No."

"He will."

"Tonight, no doubt." Carrie paused in the middle of JJ's manicure. "God, he grew up gorgeous."

"I'll say." Talia responded in the same girl-gone-foolish tone. "There's something about reformed bad boys…"

JJ fidgeted in front of the mirror. "This isn't helping my nerves."

"Oops. Sorry." Talia got control of her senses.

And so did Carrie. She flashed a chagrined expression and resumed the manicure. "Temporary lapse of judgment. It happens to the best of us."

"You don't have to tell me." JJ glanced at her ruby-colored nails. "Should I wear red lipstick? Or will that be too messy when he kisses me?"

Aaron's wife grinned. "Dylan probably likes it messy."

"*Talia.*" Thunder's fiancé scolded her.

JJ's heart went batty again. "He's probably dated a lot of women who are going to be at this party."

"Yes, but it's you he's got his eye on." Talia finished JJ's hair and stepped back to admire her handiwork. "Do you know what the past eight months were like for him? You're in his blood. He couldn't shake you if he tried."

"His intensity scares me." She waited until her nails were dry before she reached for a tube of red lipstick. Her eyes had already been shadowed with smoky colors and lined in with a smudgy black pencil.

Talia made a troubled face. "If you make love with him too soon, he'll nab you right up."

Her nerves tensed. "You make me sound doomed already."

"You were doomed the day he rescued you. But that doesn't mean you can't fight it."

"Like wearing my own dress?"

"And not letting tonight go beyond a kiss."

JJ nodded. It was a sound advice, a warning to take things slow, to keep her head on straight. But coming from a woman who'd married Dylan's equally intense cousin, it hardly mattered.

When push came to shove, the Trueno men prevailed.

"I should get my clothes on," JJ said. For now she was wearing her bra and panties with a robe. "I don't hear the maid anymore."

They went into her room and she opened the closet and removed the garment bag that contained her dress.

She unzipped it. And gasped.

Her dress was gone, and in its place was a black gown featuring fluid lines, shiny sequins and glass beads. It was the most dazzling creation JJ had ever seen.

"Dylan." Her voice all but cracked. "How could he have switched them? My dress was here earlier. You saw it. You both saw it."

"He must have paid the hotel maid to do it," Carrie said. "To time it just right."

"Yeah, and there we were, huddled in the bathroom like hens, talking about how sexy he is." Talia reached out to take the breathtaking finery, to snatch it greedily in her hands. A silk wrap came with it. "That sneaky SOB." She checked the label on the dress, moaned a little. "Hot damn. This is a vintage Madeleine Vionnet. 1930s, I'll bet. Did you know she invented the bias cut?"

Carrie moved forward. "You're siding with the enemy, Talia. Oh, my goodness. Check out the bottom of the bag. Shoes, a purse. I wonder if there's jewelry inside. A few baubles to go with the French couture."

JJ fought a wave of dizziness. She sat down and opened the beaded clutch. Sure enough, a delicate choker with iridescent pearls and matching earrings caught the light.

"Those are vintage, too. Old Hollywood." Talia leaned over her shoulder. "Now I want Aaron to buy me something."

Carrie sighed. "So do I. With Thunder, I mean." She shook her head. "I'll bet our guys knew all about this."

"Of course they did." Talia was still holding the Madeline Vionnet. "The three Musketeers."

JJ fingered the pearls. "What am I going to do?"

"Wear it. All of it. Like Cinderella," Talia told her. "Just be cautious after midnight."

JJ could barely breathe. "That I don't end up in his bed?"

Talia nodded, and they fell into an emotion-packed silence. The seduction had already begun. The antique jewelry. The glamour-girl gown.

"What if it doesn't fit?" JJ asked.

"Are you kidding? Dylan wouldn't have taken something like that to chance." Talia handed her the dress. "He probably measured every stitch of clothing you own."

"He probably remembers every curve of your body, too," Carrie said. "From when he carried you out of that awful trailer."

"From that to this." With the other's women's help, JJ zipped into the gown, slipped on the shoes and put the pearls in place, stunned by how magnificent she looked.

And by how anxious she was to see her prince.

Dylan entered the bungalow and found Julia seated on the sofa in the living room, waiting for him.

She stood and their eyes met.

He wanted to pull her into his arms, to kiss her with the kind of fever that rushed through a man's bones.

But he didn't. Not yet.

He moved closer and reached out to touch her hair. Softly, gently, twining his finger around one of the loose strands.

"It's paler," he said, cursing himself for the fairy tale reaction. "More blonde."

She nodded, her eyes still fixed on his. "Talia and Carrie lightened it for me."

"It works. With the dress, with the jewelry. It fits."

"You shouldn't have done this, Dylan. I should be angry at you."

"Because I'm Coyote?" he asked. When she gave him a confused expression, he added, "All the wicked things man does, Coyote did first."

Her breath hitched. "Is that Apache folklore?"

He nodded. "You look beautiful, Julia."

She swept her hands along her gown, hovering over the beads, over the teardrop paillettes, over a design he'd come to know intimately.

"I feel beautiful," she said.

"Wickedly beautiful?" he asked.

"Dangerously beautiful." She paused, dropped her hands. "How did you pull this off? How did you—"

"I asked the hotel concierge for help, and he recommended a stylist. A lady who shops for celebrities. I met with her yesterday morning while you were still asleep. You didn't even know I was gone." He turned, gestured to the painting of the 1930s starlet on wall. "I told her about that picture. I told her that was how I wanted you to look."

She traced the pearls at her throat, as if they were shackles, almost as if Dylan was beginning to own her. "And I do."

"Yes," he agreed. "You do."

"Giving into you scares me," she said.

"I can tell." He watched her fidget with the choker. "Maybe I'll get a tattoo with your name on it."

"What? Oh, my goodness. Don't do that. Don't connect us anymore than we are."

"My grandfather had a tattoo with my grandmother's name. In his day, the White Mountain people tattooed letters on their bodies, and he chose her name."

"They were married. She was his wife. We're—" She stalled, frowned. "I don't know what we are."

"Neither do I." He looked at her mouth, at the glossy red color. "Did you wear that lipstick for me?"

"Yes."

"Why?"

"Because you're going to kiss me tonight."

"I am?" He smiled. Captivated. Amused. "When?"

"I don't know." She met his gaze. "Probably when I least expect it." She clutched the pearls again. "Are we leaving soon?"

"I still have to get dressed." For now he was in blue jeans. "But it won't take me long to get ready." He angled his head. "By the way, I'm having another dress delivered to you tomorrow. Another necklace, too."

She sucked in her breath. "I don't want to think about another dress. Or more jewels. Or another party. I just need to get through tonight. To secure donations for the fundraiser."

"And you will. A lot of the guests are going to be curious to meet you. To talk to you." He reached out to skim her cheek, just to satisfy his craving to touch her, just to absorb the softness. "They already know how long I searched for you."

She blinked, took a step back. "You told them?"

"No, but I went AWOL for eight months. Word gets around."

"Yes, of course. It just sounds so—"

"Crazy?" he asked.

"Chivalrous," she responded.

Suddenly he frowned. Being responsible for her mother's death wasn't chivalrous. And keeping it a secret was even worse.

"Are they going to gossip about us?" she asked, jarring his thoughts.

"Who?"

"The people at the party."

"Some of them probably will." He tried to imagine how she would look after he kissed her, after her lipstick was smeared. "They'll figure out that I'm obsessed with you, too."

"Who hasn't?" she asked a little nervously, as he walked away to get dressed, to put on a suit and tie and get the evening underway.

Six

A fiftysomething blonde in a pink gown and blue diamonds hosted the party. Her name was Kathleen and she was a supermarket heiress.

Enjoying her cushy station in life, she kissed Dylan on the cheek and welcomed JJ into her home.

And what a home, JJ thought.

Kathleen's hilltop residence featured a waterfall that spilled into the pool, a sprawling tennis court and a luxurious barn that harmonized the beach-front view.

According to Dylan, Kathleen loved being rich, but she loved her horses most of all.

The Spanish-style mansion was decorated with

butter-soft leathers and carved woods. A Bolin saddle and other cowboy collectibles were flanked with silver.

The party was everywhere, all throughout the house and all over the grounds. Waiters and waitresses, dressed in gunslinger gear with batwing chaps and Hollywood holsters, offered food and drink.

JJ accepted a glass of champagne. "This is…"

"Billy the Kid meets Malibu?" Dylan took her arm and guided her down the hall. "Kathleen always has black tie parties with a western theme. It's her signature." He smiled. "I already told her about the fundraiser and hit her up for a donation. She was happy to help."

"That's wonderful. I'll be sure to thank her."

They wandered into the ballroom where a saloon-style setting had been created: poker tables already filled with gambling guests, a rustic bar with free-flowing whiskey and stairs that led to what looked like a posh bordello.

JJ noticed the individual doors. "Is that supposed to be real? Are people supposed to…"

"I think it's an old movie set. But I'm sure the beds are real. That they can be used." He paused, looked directly into her eyes, teased her the way he always did. "Do you want to go up and see them?"

JJ shook her head. She was already overwhelmed. She could feel a cluster of gracefully gowned women watching her and Dylan, waiting to see if they would ascend the stairs.

Finally a full-figured brunette approached them. She kissed Dylan on the cheek, the same way Kathleen had done, and introduced herself to JJ.

"I'm Sara," she said. "Single, sassy and always on the prowl."

Dylan rolled his eyes, and the other woman laughed.

"You used to be on the prowl, too," she told him.

He moved closer to JJ. "Not anymore."

"So I see." Unscathed, Sara winked at JJ, then checked out a passing waiter, taking a good look at his blue-jeaned butt.

On the prowl indeed.

Soon the rest of the socialites in Sara's circle gathered around them, too. JJ sensed that they weren't part of Dylan's dating pool. They were the gossip brigade she'd been worried about.

A few minutes later Dylan was whisked away by several male acquaintances, leaving JJ to her own devices.

"Did Dylan buy you that dress?" Sara asked.

"Yes, he did."

"It's beautiful." The brunette lingered over the vintage design, admiring the museum-quality detail. "I swear you've got to be the most interesting girl here."

JJ opted for modesty. Or so she hoped. "Only because Dylan rescued me from a dangerous situation."

"He's the real thing, isn't he? A cowboy. An Indian. A horse whisperer. He fascinates this crowd."

"You mean the women?" JJ asked.

"The men, too. But yes, I was referring to the women." Sara flashed a perfect white smile. She was south-of-the-border sexy with waist-length hair and breasts as big as balloons. "We've been dying to meet you."

JJ sipped her champagne, her hand not quite steady. She felt like a science experiment, a kidnapping victim in a petri dish. "Because Dylan spent all that time searching for me?"

"Totally." This came from a perky blonde. "Did you run away from him? Was he part of your escape?"

"No." She paused, remembered putting her mouth perilously close to his. "At least not consciously."

"Dylan has never looked at anyone the way he looks at you," Sara said. "Not even Linda."

Taken aback, JJ all but blinked. "Linda?"

"His longest-lasting girlfriend. She brought him to his first party. She introduced him to everyone. It was a long time ago, but something strange happened between them. They were this flirty couple, always hanging all over each other, and then boom…" The storyteller dusted her bejeweled hands, making a finished gesture. "It was over. And no one knows why."

JJ's pulse tumbled. "Is Linda here?"

A different blonde chimed in. She was tall, tan and anorexic thin. "Linda is out of town but she'll be back tomorrow. In time for the next party."

"But don't worry about her." Sara joined the conversation again. "It's you Dylan is hungry for. And he doesn't care if everyone knows it."

But what he felt for Linda was anyone's guess?

Troubled by the thought, JJ glanced up at the bordello, catching a peek of thick velvet drapes, gold braiding and rich brocades.

Sara opened her mouth to say something else, but Dylan returned and the brunette changed the subject.

Quickly. Skillfully.

As if they hadn't been talking about him at all.

Dylan guided Julia toward the garden, toward a brick-and-glass conservatory. He wanted to spend some time alone with her, amid flowers and plants and fragrant botanicals.

She seemed exceptionally quiet. She was still nursing the same glass of champagne, and her expression was distant.

They entered the environmentally controlled building where hothouse flora bloomed.

"My mom loves orchids," he said. "I guess a lot of women do."

Julia's voice went flat. "Are you fishing for my favorite flower again?"

"I don't know. Maybe." He furrowed his brows. "Are you going to tell me?"

"No." She wandered over to an ornate bench, where she sat and gazed at the view. Beyond the glass was the sea, rising and roaming from the cliffs below.

Dylan remained standing. "Did I do something to upset you?"

"No," she said again, placing her champagne glass on a mosaic table.

"Someone did."

"It's nothing." She turned, studied a yellow flower. "This is pretty."

"It's a butterfly orchid." He pointed to long slim plant with narrow leaves and fuchsia blooms. "That's a pink princess. My mom used to drive us nuts with all of this."

"Pink princess." She almost touched the delicate petals, then pulled her hand back. "Orchids have romantic names, don't they?"

"Yes, but they have scientific ones, too. Not that I can pronounce them." When she turned her attention back to the sea, he frowned. "Tell me what's wrong. Tell me why you seem so faraway."

She looked up and caught his gaze. "I want to know about Linda. I want you to tell me about her."

He started. He hadn't expected that name to come up. Not like this. "We dated. Years ago. Who mentioned her to you? Was it Sara?"

"It was all of those women. They all mentioned her."

He removed his jacket and tossed it over the arm of the bench. He was getting warm, the hothouse air stifling. "After all this time? She's no different from anyone else I dated."

"You're lying, Dylan. Sara and the others told me that something strange happened between you."

When a mister sprayed a row of flowers, he jerked from the sudden movement. "What happened between us is personal."

"Oh, really?" She stood up, meeting him eye to eye, clutching her sequined purse with all her might. "Why is my life an open book and yours personal? You know almost everything about me, and I know barely anything about you."

"I still see Linda at these parties. We still run into each other."

"Yes, I know. She'll be here tomorrow night. Is that why you wanted to bring me to California? To show me off to her?"

Stunned, he could do little more than stare. "I wanted to bring you here because this is part of my life."

"So is she."

"Not anymore. We prefer to ignore each other."

"Why?" she pressed.

"Sometimes that's what old lovers do. Sometimes it's easier than pretending to be friends." He dragged a hand through his hair. "I was twenty years old when we were together. I'm almost thirty now. I had no idea people were talking about it ten years later."

"They probably weren't. Not until you showed up with me." She all but crowded him. "The woman you're obsessed with."

He crowded her right back. "I've dated a slew of

socialites since Linda. No one is supposed to give a damn. Not about her. It's us that matters."

She pierced his gaze. "There is no us, Dylan. It's all in your mind."

"Oh, yeah. Is this in my mind?" Without a second thought, he grabbed her.

And kissed her.

She tried to pull away, but he held on, forcing her to give in. He could feel her heart pounding, racing in fear, in excitement, in anticipation.

Finally her mouth opened beneath his, and he plundered, rough and carnal, with sexual juices spiraling through his veins.

She struggled for her next breath, but he didn't care. He pushed her against the wall and imagined crashing through the glass.

She clawed his shoulders, and the mister changed direction, hitting the back of his shirt.

He used his tongue, over and over, deepening the kiss, taking it to the limit.

He wanted to shred her gown, to scatter the shiny ornaments like stars, to make dark, desperate love to her.

But he stopped himself before he went too far.

He jerked back, leaving her where she was, pressed against the conservatory, against the insanity he'd created.

"I expected you to kiss me tonight," she said. "But you shouldn't have done it like that."

"Too late." He cursed the night stalker he was

turning out to be. "I already did." Her lipstick wasn't smeared. He'd eaten it clean off. He could taste the waxy flavor.

He used the back of his hand to wipe his mouth, and she started fussing with her dress, checking for damaged beads, for broken sequins.

"It's fine," he told her, thinking how fragile she looked, how impossibly beautiful. "I didn't ruin it. I wanted to, but I didn't."

"It felt like…"

"We were falling? Like everything was shattering?"

"Yes." She hesitated, glanced around for her purse, found it on the ground, where she must have dropped it midkiss. "I need some air." She gulped the last of her champagne and headed for the door, warning him not to follow.

He didn't listen.

She moved at a quickened pace. Above her head, strands of tiny white lights twined in and out of trees, making twinkling shapes.

"Are you cold?" he asked, as the wind turned sharp. She'd left her wrap in the cloakroom of Kathleen's mansion.

She shook her head. "The last thing I want is to wear your jacket. So don't you dare offer it to me."

When she tried to move past him, he caught her arm. "Slow down, Julia."

"Why? So you can kiss me again?" Her heels echoed on the flagstone path.

"Yes."

She stopped. "What?"

"I said yes."

Only this time he did it slowly, tenderly, making the feather-light feeling last.

She didn't pull away. She all but melted against him, like a gothic candle dripping wax.

He went hard, heady, a jumble of heat, of heartbeat. He couldn't remember ever feeling this good, this confused, this erotically annoyed with a woman. Desire swirled like a drug, like the kind of addiction that was bound to make him a junkie.

When he came up for air, for the oxygen they both needed, she swayed on her feet. He caught her before she fell, latching onto her wrists, balancing her with cuffed hands.

"I should slap you," she said, breaking free.

"Go ahead," he challenged.

She walked toward the cliff instead, where ivy tangled around a metal guardrail.

Dylan went with her. Her predator. Her protector. He watched every move she made.

The loose strands of her hair blew in the wind, as untamed as the sea, as the ocean crashing on the sand.

"What does Linda look like?" she asked.

He shook his head, snarled a little, wondered why she couldn't let it go. "You'll see her tomorrow night." A twig snapped under his foot, under his weight. "I'm sure Sara will point her out."

"I want to know what she looks like now." She made a disconcerting expression. Hurt. Anger. Riddled emotion. "Is she a blonde? A brunette?"

He heaved an exasperated sigh. "She's a redhead."

"Natural or dyed?"

He raised his eyebrows, gave her a you've-got-to-be-kidding look.

"Natural or dyed?" she asked again. She was serious.

"Natural."

"Were you in love with her?"

"Christ," he said.

"Don't cuss." She paused, persisted. "Were you?"

"No, damn it, I wasn't."

"Are you sure?"

"Yes." He wasn't foolish enough to think that hard-shelled men didn't fall in love. He'd seen it happen to his brother, to his cousin. But this was different. "I'm positive." He reached for her hand. "Let's go back to the party."

"That's it?" She scowled at him. "You're done talking?"

"Yes," he told her, shutting her up with another kiss—a quick hot blast of tongue and teeth, taking what he wanted, what he needed.

What he couldn't help but crave.

Seven

The party ended and when JJ and Dylan returned to the hotel at 1:00 a.m., she couldn't think of anything to say.

And apparently neither could he.

He unlocked their bungalow with the card key and escorted her inside. She flipped on the light and illuminated the living room.

He tossed his jacket on the sofa, and she studied him. His tie was undone and his features looked as if they'd been sculpted from kiln-baked clay. Angular, she thought. Hard-edged handsome.

She waited for him to release his hair, to undo the ponytail, but he didn't. He left it the way it was, combed strikingly away from his face and bound with an old-fashioned leather queue.

When he pierced her gaze, when the air around them went thick, JJ panicked.

"Talia warned me not to sleep with you tonight," she said, her voice cutting into the clock-choked silence.

"Since when does Talia make decisions for you?" He moved closer, close enough to slam her heart into the back of her throat.

JJ removed her wrap and fisted the silk, clutching it in front of her, using it like a shield. "She doesn't."

"I didn't expect you to be with me tonight, not after everything that happened."

"You didn't?"

"I want you, Julia. God, how I want you." He tipped her chin and looked into her eyes, making her shiver, making her breath catch. "But I know you're not ready. Things are strange between us."

Her wrap slid to the floor, pooling like the midnight silk that it was. "Things were strange between you and Linda."

His gaze went cold. "That was different."

She stepped back, leaving the filmy fabric at his feet. "I want you to tell me about her. Tomorrow morning. When we both have a clear head."

"We'll see." He picked up her wrap, draped it over a chair and walked to his room.

Leaving her alone and waiting for daybreak.

JJ went to bed, and when the sun rose in the sky,

she got up and got ready, taking a shower and clipping her towel-dried hair with a big gold barrette, making a rooster-style ponytail out of it.

Needing a cup of coffee, she went into the kitchen, where daylight filtered into the room, raining on the hushed appliances.

Footsteps caught her attention and she spun around to find Dylan in the doorway. He hadn't showered yet. His hair was long and messy, and he wore a pair of pale blue pajama bottoms. His chest was bare, his nipples brown and erect.

"Coffee?" she asked.

He nodded. "And breakfast, too."

"Should I order room service?"

"No. I asked the hotel to stock the fridge." He leaned against the doorway. Brooding masculinity at its finest. "So you could cook for me."

She cursed his proximity, his rumpled-male appeal. "Like a housekeeper?"

"Or a mistress." He slanted her a smart-aleck smile. "Or a wife. I'm not picky. I just want a home-cooked meal."

She wasn't in the mood for his games, for his seduction. She could still taste his kisses from the night before. "Don't be smug."

"Why do my marriage jokes bother you?" He cocked his head, considered her. "Is it because your old boyfriends are married?"

"No." She made the coffee, but she was still debating breakfast. "I got over Dan ages ago."

"What about Gilbert?"

She removed two hotel-monogrammed mugs from the cupboard. "Gilbert was ages ago, too. A few years after Dan."

"I know. Thunder interviewed him."

"The way he interviewed Dan? Please tell me our sex life didn't come up."

"It didn't. Gilbert's wife was there. Thunder said they seemed happy."

"I'm glad." Her relationship with Gilbert had fizzled out. No heat. No spark. Mundane masculinity at its worst. "We're supposed to be talking about you, Dylan. About Linda."

"Yes, of course." His smile fell. "My illustrious girlfriend. The woman who aborted my child."

JJ almost dropped the cup in her hand. "There was a baby?" She hadn't envisioned him as father. Not even an almost-father.

He was still standing in the doorway. "It's a long story."

"I have time."

"Then fix me breakfast."

She agreed, but only to get him to step farther into the kitchen. He did, frowning the entire time. He sat at the table and she gave him his coffee. By now she knew that he liked it black.

He tasted the scalding drink. "I'm not the daddy

type, but when Linda did what she did…" He hesitated, let his words fade. "She said it was her body, her choice. I didn't even know there was a baby until it was gone, until it was over."

JJ had no idea how to comfort him or if even he wanted her to. His voice was flat, devoid of emotion.

He didn't say anything else, so she started the meal, making cheese omelets, hash browns and bacon. When she turned to look at him, she saw that he was watching her.

Self-conscious, she put bread in the toaster. She wouldn't have aborted his baby. But she wouldn't have gotten pregnant by him, either. Not by a man who wasn't her husband. JJ didn't take those kinds of chances.

When the food was ready, she put it on the table with butter, jelly and ketchup. Then she sat across from him.

He looked past the condiments at her. "Do you want kids?"

"Yes, I do. Someday," she added. "When the time is right."

"I never did. But I never expected to lose a child, either."

When he cut into his eggs, his fork made a scraping sound. "Did you know that Carrie and Thunder lost a baby? The first time they were married?"

She sat forward in her chair. "No, I didn't."

"Carrie had a miscarriage. I remember when it

happened. I was just a kid, but it affected me, too. It was the first time I'd ever seen my brother cry."

JJ's heart went soft, sad. "Did you cry when Linda took away your baby?"

He shook his head. "I was too—" He added ketchup to his hashed browns, making a blood-red mess. "Numb."

Because there was more to the story, so much more. But he was already clamming up, already giving her limited information. "You're a good secret keeper, aren't you, Dylan?"

He glanced up from his plate, but he didn't respond.

"Does your family know about your baby?" she asked.

"I didn't see any point in telling them. I moved on with my life."

But he didn't, she thought. He hadn't moved on. Not completely. And in some odd way, JJ was part of it. Part of him and Linda.

Part of what he'd lost.

Part of whatever it was Dylan was trying to regain.

After breakfast JJ cleared the table, and Dylan disappeared to take a shower.

She was still contemplating the Linda situation when a knock sounded at the door. Unsure of what to expect, she answered it.

"Good morning, ma'am." A young man from the hotel staff handed her a package with her name on it.

"Thank you." She removed a few dollars from her purse, tipped him and carried the cumbersome box into the living room, assuming it was her dress for tonight.

Anxious to see it, she got a steak knife and sawed through the edges of the tape. By the time she got to the contents of the box, her curiosity was beyond piqued.

She unwrapped the tissue and discovered a voluminous floor-length skirt. Made from yards of a satiny blue fabric, it bunched in her hands. The matching blouse was high-necked and full-sleeved. Both garments were trimmed with rows of ornamental braid.

A necklace fashioned from silver and abalone shell completed the ensemble, along with cowboy boots and a complementary purse.

JJ loved it. The beauty. The ladylike modesty. The Native and western flair.

Dylan came into the living room with damp hair and wearing comfy-looking jeans.

She glanced up at him. "This is beautiful. Where did you find it?"

"It's what Apache women on the rez wore in the 1940s," he said. "It belonged to my grandmother. The dress did, anyway. The accessories are new."

JJ went speechless. He'd given her a family heirloom.

What?" he said, questioning the gaping expression on her face.

The Silhouette Reader Service™ — Here's how it works:

Accepting your 2 free books and 2 free mystery gifts places you under no obligation to buy anything. You may keep the books and gifts and return the shipping statement marked "cancel." If you do not cancel, about a month later we'll send you 6 additional books and bill you just $3.80 each in the U.S., or $4.47 each in Canada, plus 25¢ shipping and handling per book and applicable taxes if any.* That's the complete price and — compared to cover prices of $4.50 each in the U.S. and $5.25 each in Canada — it's quite a bargain! You may cancel at any time, but if you choose to continue, every month we'll send you 6 more books, which you may either purchase at the discount price or return to us and cancel your subscription.

*Terms and prices subject to change without notice. Sales tax applicable in N.Y. Canadian residents will be charged applicable provincial taxes and GST. All orders subject to approval. Credit or debit balances in a customer's account(s) may be offset by any other outstanding balance owed by or to the customer. Please allow 4 to 6 weeks for delivery.

BUSINESS REPLY MAIL
FIRST-CLASS MAIL   PERMIT NO. 717-003   BUFFALO, NY

POSTAGE WILL BE PAID BY ADDRESSEE

SILHOUETTE READER SERVICE
3010 WALDEN AVE
PO BOX 1867
BUFFALO NY 14240-9952

NO POSTAGE
NECESSARY
IF MAILED
IN THE
UNITED STATES

She regained her senses. "I can't wear your grandmother's dress to a party."

"Why not?"

"Because it's special. It's—"

He cut her off. "It's not real satin. It's an imitation fabric."

She held the blouse against her body. "I wasn't talking about its monetary value."

"My mom has a trunk full of Grandma's old stuff. She didn't mind giving this to you." He sat on the edge of an ottoman, straddling it in male fashion. "When the stylist was searching for gowns, I called Mom and asked her if she thought any of Grandma's dresses would work. The stylist thought it was a great idea, too."

Her heart was spinning. "I don't know what to say."

"Say you'll wear it. We rushed to get it here in time, to alter it for you."

She fingered the ornamental braid, the hand-sewn detail. "It doesn't look like it's from the 1940s."

"That's because it was old-fashioned for its day. Apache women weren't wearing what other women were wearing in the forties. They were still wearing a style that was adopted by white women in the 1800s. For everyday and for special occasions."

And he was fascinated by his ancestors, she thought. He was more Apache than he gave himself credit for. "Is this the grandma whose husband had her name tattooed on his body?"

He nodded. "Her name was Mary. He was crazy about her."

"I can only imagine how lovely she must have been."

"Will you wear her dress?"

She met his gaze, those deep, dark eyes. "Yes."

"The stylist suggested that we modernize it a bit, so that's why the accessories are new. My mom made the necklace."

She fingered the abalone shells, the silver beads. "I'll be sure to thank her, to tell her how much this means to me."

"The boots are a modern touch, too. Grandma wore moccasins for special occasions. When she did her chores, she went barefoot. Life was hard back then. Women were still carrying their kids around in cradleboards." Suddenly he frowned, the enthusiasm drifting from his voice.

An uncomfortable reminder that his ex-girlfriend had aborted his child, JJ thought.

When a dark cloud befell them, she shifted on the sofa, unsure of what to do, of what to say.

Finally, she went back to the boots. "I like this brand."

"So do I," he responded automatically.

"Is this another western-themed party?"

He nodded. "But it isn't black tie. It's more of a country get-together, I guess. I'll be wearing cowboy clothes, too."

Later that night, he lived up to his claim. They got

ready to go out, and he donned a white shirt, a leather vest and a turquoise-and-silver bolo tie. His hair was bound with a brightly colored silk scarf, an item that had belonged to his grandfather.

He looked beautiful. Completely in his element.

They drove to an equestrian castle located near state and county parks. The land was lush and green and rife with trees.

The party was on the lawn, where a man-made lake glistened. An outdoor arena, a hot walker and custom-built paddocks accommodated show-quality horses.

A stage had been erected for a country band, and a gourmet chef was in charge of the buffet-style barbecue.

The homeowners, a thirty-something couple with quick wit and nouveau money, welcomed Dylan with open arms.

April, the wife, a western artist absorbed in Native history, raved over JJ's outfit, especially when she discovered that it had belonged to Dylan's grandmother.

She touched the fabric lovingly. "It makes you proud to be a woman, doesn't it?"

JJ nodded. "I'm honored to have something like this."

"I can see why." The artist glanced at Dylan, who was chatting amicably with her husband. "Dylan already told us about your fundraiser. I'd love to get involved. Maybe auction off one of my paintings."

"Thank you so much. That would be amazing."

"What's amazing is Dylan rescuing you from a kidnapping, then going ballistic to find you after you disappeared. How sexy is that? Everyone is talking about you. This is your fifteen minutes of fame." She leaned in close. "You might as well make the most of it. Work this crowd for as much as you can get."

Over the next few hours JJ took April's advice and focused on raising money for the Rocking Horse Refuge and inviting people to the fundraiser, explaining that it was a family event and that they could bring their children. She'd learned that a lot of the guests—divorced, married or otherwise—had kids, with green-card nannies to look after them.

But not Linda. She hadn't kept Dylan's baby.

Every so often, JJ glanced around, trying to figure out who she was.

So far she hadn't seen a redhead who fit the bill, at least not in her mind.

Nor had she come across Sara or the other women who'd told her about Linda. She assumed they hadn't arrived yet.

"Do you want to dance?" Dylan asked.

JJ blinked, turned, looked at her date. Apparently he hadn't figured out that she was scouting the grounds for his old girlfriend. Or maybe he did, and he was trying to distract her. She couldn't be sure.

"Yes, thank you," she said, sounding a bit too polite. "That would be nice."

The music was soft and easy. Other couples gathered on the grass, swaying to the made-for-lovers beat.

Dylan took JJ in his arms, and she inhaled the musk-and-lavender richness of his cologne, the familiar fragrance that wrapped itself around her as sensuously as his embrace.

She forgot about Linda.

Temporary insanity, she thought.

When Dylan kissed her, her limbs went mushy.

His tongue teased hers, and she leaned forward, letting him bring her closer. They moved in time to the song, back and forth.

Heat. Desire. Fodder for gossip.

His hips bumped hers, and her skirt swished against his fly.

"You feel good," he whispered.

"You feel better," she whispered back, knowing she was losing what was left of her mind.

He kissed her again, claiming her, letting everyone know that the runaway girl belonged to him.

JJ should have stopped him, but she didn't. She allowed the warmth, the mouth-tingling wetness, the public intimacy to sweep her away.

They succumbed to two more ballads. He moved his hands lower, catching her waist, and she looped her arms around his neck.

Their bodies were almost airtight now.

"Did you ever go to school dances?" she asked.

He nuzzled her cheek. "Where the chaperones made you stop doing what we're doing?"

She nodded, felt his breath stroke her skin.

"I always got in trouble," he said.

"I can't imagine why."

He smiled and turned his face to kiss her again. He couldn't get enough, she realized. He wanted more. He wanted every naughty schoolboy taste of her.

She imagined him doing other orally fixated things to her, and she flushed under her own fantasy.

And then the music ended. Just like that, the band quit playing.

Awkward as can be, Dylan and JJ separated.

"What happened?" she asked.

"They're taking break," he responded, as if the musicians had betrayed them.

For a moment, the party seemed to be spinning, the lawn, the trees, the other guests whirring past her.

"I could use a drink," he said.

"Me, too."

She got her sea legs back, and they found the nearest portable bar. But the line was horrendous.

"Tell me what you want, and I'll get it," he told her.

"White wine," she decided.

He infiltrated the throng of waiting-to-be-served drinkers, getting in several conversations with people he knew along the way.

JJ watched him, then turned and spotted a tall, slim, fair-skinned woman. She wore jeweled chains around her boots and a diamond-studded band around her Stetson. Irish red hair dazzled from beneath the hat.

Their gazes locked from across the yard.

Dead on.

JJ knew she was Linda.

Eight

Linda moved forward and JJ realized the other woman was heading toward her.

To say hello? To introduce herself?

No, JJ thought. Linda's paces were strong and determined, with her head held high. This was a confrontation.

JJ squared her shoulders and moved forward, too. What else could she do? Turn and walk way? Fade into the shadows? She hadn't done anything wrong. Dating Dylan wasn't a crime.

They met halfway, coming face to face in the middle of the yard, with the party buzzing around them. The deep-pit barbecue sent mesquite-seasoned flavors into the air, and pole-mounted floodlights struck an incandescent glow.

For what seemed like a long drawn-out moment, they simply looked at each other.

Taut. Silent.

Linda lifted her chin, and the diamonds at her ears flashed in the artificial light. She had fine-boned features and a regal quality. Her eyes were an overly vibrant shade of green. JJ suspected tinted contacts lens.

Her nails were fake, too. She bared them like badger claws.

"I can tell that Dylan told you about me," she finally said. "I can see it on your face."

"Yes he did. But only after I questioned him."

The other woman pursed her lips. "So what exactly did he say?"

JJ glanced in Dylan's direction, but didn't see him. He was in the bar line somewhere. "He told me what happened."

"What I did?"

"Yes." Even though no one was close enough to eavesdrop, she wasn't about to say "baby" or "abortion" out loud.

And apparently neither was Linda.

The socialite removed a pack of cigarettes from her shoulder bag and tapped them against her wrist. "Did he tell you about our game? Our unholy alliance? Or did he keep those dirty little details to himself?"

JJ released a swift breath. Suddenly her mind was reeling, spinning in sordid circles. "He didn't tell me everything."

"You should ask him about it." The redhead clicked a fancy gold lighter, lit a cigarette and took a dramatic puff. "You should get the whole story."

A cluster of partygoers laughed in the distance and the sound drifted cheerily, making this conversation seem surreal.

The smell of mentholated tobacco hit the air. "Does he still hate me?"

JJ started. "What?"

"Dylan."

She looked into the other woman's color-enhanced eyes and saw them ice over. "Do you still hate him?"

"Yes."

"Then why does it matter?"

"Because what I did wasn't easy."

The abortion. The baby. The words they kept avoiding. "I'm sorry. I can't imagine—"

Linda waved away her sympathy. "I'm not saying that I spent the last ten years mourning my decision. I haven't. But sometimes it still hurts."

JJ couldn't help herself. She defended the father. "It hurt him, too."

Linda stamped out her barely-smoked cigarette, grinding it beneath her boot, leaving the butt in the grass. "Because our stupid little game blew up in his face. And in mine," she added, her voice fading a little. "My mother took me to the clinic that day. I was nineteen years old and crying my eyes out. Dylan Trueno was the worst thing that ever happened to me." She paused, sighed. "But maybe you'll have better luck. Maybe it'll work out for you."

"I'm not—" JJ stopped in mid-sentence, unsure of what to say.

"Falling in love with him?" Linda had the gall to smile. "You'll probably end up hating him, too."

God, she hoped not. With her defenses down, she wasn't able to decipher her emotions, to make sense of them. "Were you in love with him?"

"Me? Heavens, no. I wanted his brother."

"Thunder?" JJ's heart lurched, lunged, fell flat to the ground.

"Don't look so shocked. Thunder wasn't married at the time. He'd been divorced for quite a while."

"But he was part of the game?"

"Are you kidding? Thunder *was* the game."

God forbid. "Are you over him?"

"Who? Thunder?" Linda reached for another cigarette, identifying herself as a chain smoker. "Totally. Completely. But that doesn't excuse what happened between Dylan and me. It doesn't make it all right."

"No, I suspect that it doesn't. But I'll wait to hear his side of the story."

"You do that, sugar. But when he cons you into his

bed, if you aren't sleeping with him already, don't say that I didn't warn you."

With that said, Linda walked away. Just in time for JJ to look over her shoulder.

And see Dylan coming toward her with their drinks.

Dylan had a pretty good idea of what had just gone down. He'd seen enough to figure things out. Especially after Linda stormed off, probably leaving unanswered questions in Julia's mind.

Secrets, scandals and lies, he thought.

The melodrama of his life.

He shouldn't have brought Julia to this party. But he hadn't expected Linda to cause a scene. Not after ten years of keeping silent.

He approached Julia and handed her a clear plastic cup. "Your wine," he managed to say. "And my beer." He lifted the foaming draft brew.

She gave him a troubled look. "What are you toasting? Your past? The game you and Linda played with your brother?"

He lowered his cup. "I wasn't toasting anything. I was just—" He brought it to his lips and guzzled. There wasn't enough alcohol to give him a mind-numbing buzz, but he did his best.

"Tell me the truth, Dylan. Tell me what happened."

The air crackled with tension. He was starting to hate this town and everything it represented. "Not here. Not in the middle of the damn barbecue."

"Then somewhere else. Somewhere quieter."

"Like the nearest guillotine?" So his head could be lobbed off? So it could roll into a Malibu ditch?

"If that's what it takes. I told Linda I would reserve judgment until I heard your side of the story."

He indicated the opposite side of the riding arena, where the other guests would fade into the distance. She agreed to the out-of-the-way location, and they trekked across the manicured grass.

He could've used another beer. But he curbed his need to get rip roaring drunk and threw away his empty cup. Julia still hadn't touched her wine. Not one commiserating sip.

By the time they reached the pristine white fence that enclosed the arena, he took comfort in the horse-and-hay smell. The paddocks were downwind.

"I met Linda at Thunder's office," he said. "Ten years ago. Here in L.A. I was visiting my brother, and he introduced us. He knew her through her family. They'd hired him for some investigative work."

Julia fired off her first question. "Was he attracted to her?"

Dylan shook his head. "He treated her like a kid. The way he treated me. The age difference between us was more apparent back then. He was this big bad mercenary, this global security specialist, this former military man, and I was his *little* brother. God, how I hated that."

The interview continued. The Cain and Abel interrogation. "You were envious of Thunder?"

"I loved my brother. I still do." He paused, fought the discomfort that came with being honest. "But at the time I was hungry for the kind of women he attracted. Rich, gorgeous society girls."

Julia's expression soured. "Like Linda?"

"Yes, like her. She was perfect for me. Or so I thought." He dug his heels into the grass, into the dirt. "We had horses in common. I was an up-and-coming trainer, gaining statewide notoriety, and she had a barn full of ribbons and trophies. She'd been competing since she was a child."

Julia finally sipped her wine. But she didn't blade him with another question. She didn't dig the knife any deeper. She remained quiet, waiting for him to continue.

Her tactic worked. He confessed on his own. "It was fun for a while. The game, as Linda called it. She wanted Thunder, and I wanted her." The wind stirred, snapping a lone leaf on the ground. "I told her I could make her forget all about my brother. That I was just as exciting as he was."

"And that's how it got started?"

He nodded. "But Linda had a different agenda. She thought that if she dated me, Thunder would notice her. That it would spark some sort of contest."

She raised her eyebrows, seemed to get suspicious of his brother, of him, of what they were capable of. "Did it?"

He shook his head. "Thunder wouldn't have considered competing with me. Not unless it was over Carrie. She's the only woman he would have fought for, and I wouldn't have made a play for her."

Julia's demeanor softened. "Thunder was still in love with his wife?"

"Ex-wife," he corrected. "Not that he would have admitted it at the time, but that's why he slept around so much. To try to forget her."

"I can see why they're getting married again."

"Yeah, me, too." Dylan stopped talking and took a moment to study his companion. She was standing next to the fence, looking soft and beautiful in his grandmother's dress. Maidenly, he thought. Innocent. He wanted to reach out, to touch her, to hold her, but he snagged a hand through his hair instead, catching the edge of his grandfather's ancient scarf.

"What happened?" she asked. "How did your relationship with Linda progress?"

"I kept pursuing her, and she kept hoping my brother would notice her. Sometimes he used to come to these parties, too. And when he did, Linda hung all over me."

"And no one figured it out? Not Sara or any of the gossipy types?"

"No. To everyone else, Linda and I were a legitimate couple. Besides, I was determined to make things real, to win the game." He paused, squinted. "She kept saying that she wasn't going to sleep with me, but—"

"You seduced her?" Julia's mouth thinned into a disapproving line.

He got defensive. "So what if I did? The sex was good. Damn good," he punctuated, recalling all of those lustfully wrong, sin-drenched, screwed-up nights. "We had chemistry in bed."

"I'll bet." She went ramrod straight. "Did you court her the way you're courting me? Did you buy her pretty clothes? Did you make her dizzy on the dance floor?"

"Don't do that. Don't confuse the present with the past." He eased up. He wasn't spoiling for a fight. "It's different with you. I'm not pursuing you because of my brother."

"Carrie thinks you grew up gorgeous. And so does Talia."

"Really?" He held her gaze, smiled, hoped she was giving him some leeway.

She didn't return his smile. Instead she blindsided him with another accusation. "Linda hates you for getting her pregnant."

His excuse was pitched, paltry. "We got careless. We messed up with the protection."

"That isn't what she's blaming you for. It's getting her into bed in the first place."

His throat went tight. He wasn't the Big Bad Wolf. He hadn't taken advantage of Little Red Linda Hood. "Am I supposed to feel sorry for her? The woman who wished, even when we were in bed, that I was my brother? Why do you think we had so much chemistry? In the dark, I could have been him."

"I think she knew exactly who you were, Dylan. I think she knew she was losing the game. That she'd let it go too far."

"Is that why she couldn't wait to run right out and get rid of my kid?"

They fell silent. One moment became several.

Then Julia said, "That was difficult for her. She told me how hard it was."

His throat tightened all over again, and when he cleared it, his chest rumbled like a lawnmower blowing back weeds. "And now you're defending her?"

"I'm just trying to see it from her perspective."

"After I found out what she did, after she admitted it, I felt empty. Alone. Like I had this yawning hole inside me." He made a fist, pounded the vicinity of his heart. "I never wanted kids, but that baby had been mine. *Mine*," he reiterated, wishing the memory hadn't resurfaced, wishing he didn't give a damn.

"Is that the only thing that has ever truly belonged to you?" Julia asked, much too compassionate.

"I don't know. I—" He stalled and looked at her. Really looked at her. "You belonged to me. The day I rescued you. It felt like you were mine."

"Dylan—"

He cut her off, softly, gently. "You still do. You still are. You've always been mine."

Suddenly JJ couldn't stop herself. She reached out to skim his jaw, to touch him.

Because she understood. She'd figured out the connection between her and Dylan and what Linda had done. She knew what Dylan was trying to regain.

The void he was trying to fill.

"When I disappeared, I left another hole inside you," she said. "The same emptiness."

He shook his head, scowled, pulled away a little. "Don't get Freudian. Don't start analyzing me. I'm not into that."

"Why? Because it makes you uncomfortable? Don't you see why you went crazy to find me?"

He features twisted, his expression turned wary. "You're comparing yourself to—"

"I'm comparing myself to how the abortion made you feel. You couldn't stand to relive the past. To lose something else that belonged to you." She paused, caught herself, rebuffed what he'd said earlier. "Not that I do, not that I ever did."

"Like hell. What about the way you almost kissed me?" he shot back. "You're as guilty as I am. You're responsible for what's happening between us, too."

"You're right, I am." Denying it would be unfair. "For more than just that near-kiss. When my mother suggested that we run away, I was anxious to go. And not just because of the loan sharks."

"You were running away from me, too? From the way I affected you?"

She nodded, finished her wine, felt the alcohol sluice through her veins. "People have been asking me all along. Did you run away from Dylan? Was he part of it? And I keep saying 'not consciously.' But it *was* conscious. I just didn't want to admit it."

His eyes turned dark. "And now you have."

Her breath clogged her throat. "Yes."

He reached for her arm and pulled her closer, body to body, pulse to pulse. "You're not leaving me again." His voice went sharp. "Not ever."

It was too late to rely on logic or caution or anything else that would keep her away from him. He was already weaving his spur-a-woman magic, his warrior voodoo.

The way he'd been doing all along.

"I want to make love with you." He circled her waist, caught her hips, brought her even closer. "More than ever."

Her skirt crinkled, the fabric bunching in satiny folds. "I want that, too," she heard herself say.

"Tonight?" he asked.

"Yes."

"My Julia," he whispered.

"JJ," she countered lightly, and made him smile. They both knew that she'd accepted him calling her by her old name.

Not that she should have given in. But men like Dylan took their aggressive toll. She'd been warned.

By Talia and Carrie.

And by Linda, she thought, her stomach knotting, her muscles going rigid.

"What's wrong?" he asked, aware that she'd tensed.

"Nothing." She put her head on his shoulder and burrowed into his body. His old girlfriend didn't count. Not now. Not when JJ and Dylan were on the verge of becoming lovers.

He smoothed a hand down her hair. Gently. Protectively. "Are you sure?"

She lifted her head. She knew he cared about her. He'd chased her to the ends of the earth. He tried to save her from a hit man. And her mother, too. "Everything's fine."

"Are you hungry? It looks like the buffet is ready." He indicated the faraway line that was forming.

JJ nodded. She would take whatever sustenance she could get.

He led her toward the barbecue, holding her hand, entwining his fingers with hers.

They got in line, waited for their food, then sat at a table with Sara and her friends, who'd arrived just in time to eat.

No one gossiped, at least not outwardly. Sara hinted, albeit silently, that Linda was nearby, shooting a look in the redhead's direction. Linda was sitting several tables away.

JJ refused to acknowledge her. She focused on her meal instead, on meat smoldering with spices and side dishes brimming with exotic ingredients. She speared a hearts of palm from her salad and saw Dylan butter his bread.

He glanced up at from his plate, and their gazes locked.

As intimately as the situation would allow.

She could feel the other guests at their table watching them. Maybe even Linda, too. But it didn't matter. Because JJ and Dylan had cleared the air.

Exposing secrets.

And softening her heart.

Nine

JJ was supposed to be prepared, relaxed, ready. But the drive back to the bungalow made her nervous. Suddenly she couldn't think clearly.

"I'm not good at this," she said.

Dylan changed lanes. The weekend traffic was heavy, with vehicles curving along the canyon. "Good at what? Riding in rental cars? Listening to the radio? You're just sitting there, Julia."

"You know what I mean."

"You're worried about going to the hotel?" He slanted her a boyish smile. "We've been there for four days. You should be used to it by now."

"Exactly. You have your bed and I have mine." She

looked out the window and followed the road, the twirling, twining asphalt jungle. "Which one are we supposed to use? Am I supposed to put on a pretty nightgown and come to your room? Or are you supposed to—?"

"Strip you the minute we get in the door?" His smile peaked. "That works for me."

"Dylan." She laughed, shook her head, felt marginally better. She liked his sense of humor.

After they both went quiet he said, "I can't wait for it to happen."

She turned, gazed at his profile. The car was dim, the outline of his features illuminated, but only slightly, by the overhead glare of streetlights.

"It's all I can think about." His voice went rough. "Being inside you."

JJ's skin turned hot, humid, sweetly sticky. She considered blasting the air conditioner, but she was afraid to move, to break the spell, so she kept looking at him. He captured her imagination, all of him—the masculine beauty that made him her fantasy, the possessive hunger that made him her reality.

He got to the bottom of the canyon and stopped at a red light. She took a daring chance and put her hand on his thigh.

He all but shuddered.

Then he captured her hand, moved it to his zipper and kissed her.

A kaleidoscope exploded beneath her eyes—a

prism of color, a flash of heat, a blast of desire. She cupped the hardness in the front of his pants, and he practically devoured her in one fell swoop.

His mouth was everywhere, all over hers.

Until a horn honked.

He flinched, jerked, cursed. The light had changed.

JJ sucked a long, lethal breath into her lungs. She couldn't believe what she'd just done.

"You're dangerous," he said, gunning the gas.

She glanced at his fly. "So are you."

He leaned over, but he didn't kiss her. This time he nuzzled her cheek, his lips grazing her skin. "Maybe we should just do it in the car. I can pull over somewhere."

Was he teasing? She hoped so. "I'm willing to wait for the hotel."

"Oh, yeah?" He nipped her jaw, went back to the road. "What about whose room, whose bed and all that?"

She was still a little nervous, still unsure of herself, but she tried not to let it show. "We can just do what comes natural."

What came natural was infinite tenderness. When they were alone in the bungalow, he wrapped her in his arms.

"My room," he whispered, making the decision. "My bed."

She nodded, and he swept her up and carried her, stirring deep-seated memories.

She almost cried. Winsome tears. The girl who'd been kidnapped. The woman who'd been rescued.

With the lights turned low, he set her on her feet, and she saw the condoms, the shiny packets, on his nightstand. "Did you buy those here?"

"Here? You mean in California?" He shook his head. "I brought them with me. From home."

When he lit a braided bundle, a dried plant of some kind, she realized that he'd brought a Native herb, too. The aromatic plant coiled from the flame, emitting a vanilla scent.

"That smells good," she said.

"It's sweet grass." He came forward and removed her necklace, making the shells rattle, creating an indigenous sound.

When he reached for the buttons on her blouse, she held onto him for support. "I'm getting light-headed." From him, what he was doing.

He discarded her blouse, exposed her bra and pushed the straps off her shoulders. "You can lie down once I get you…"

Naked, she thought.

He stripped her, of her clothes, of her trying-to-stay-strong emotions, leaving her vulnerable to his touch.

She sat on the edge of the bed and looked up at him. He still wore his shirt, his vest, his pants, even his boots. He hadn't removed one stitch of his clothing.

Her pulse beat beneath her breast.

"I'm just going to hold you," he said.

"For how long?"

He nudged her down. "For as long as it takes."

He was calming her, she thought. Letting her glide into the moment. He kissed her. He caressed her, up and down, all over.

JJ reached for the scarf that bound his hair, and the fabric slid, soft and silky, into her hands. It was part of him, part of the mystical night he'd created: the low-burning lights, the sweet grass, the melting sensations.

She closed her eyes, and he said something about orchids, about butterflies and pink princesses. Naughty boy, she thought. He had his fingers between her legs.

Just resting there, teasing her, making her want more, making her dreamy.

"I feel like I'm caught on a cloud." She opened her eyes. "With a cowboy."

He tugged at her earlobe, gently, sweetly, using his teeth. "Then that must make you an angel."

"Angels don't—"

"Sure they do." He rolled over on top of her, his belt buckle imprinting her stomach.

"Are you going to get naked now?" she asked, his scarf drifting to the floor.

He didn't respond. But when he unhooked his buckle, she watched him.

Closely.

He sat up, discarded his vest and removed his shirt and bolo tie. Then he kicked off his boots and toed off his socks. By the time he got to his pants, JJ itched to touch him.

All that was left was his boxers.

She chewed her lip. "I like—"

"What?" he asked.

"This." She traced his abs, skimming the muscles like stones rippling across water.

"What about this?" He pushed her hand down farther, right into his shorts.

She connected with his penis.

He smiled.

JJ smiled, too. How enticing could a man be?

She curled her fingers around him, and he kissed her. And then they rolled over the bed, bunching sheets and wrecking havoc on pillows.

When his boxers were heaped in a pile with the rest of his clothes, he rubbed against her.

Flesh to flesh.

He buried his face against her throat, and she inhaled the scent of his skin. A sound escaped him. A groan. A primal need. She knew how badly he wanted her.

But he didn't reach for a condom.

Not yet.

He lifted her arms above her head and encouraged her to hold onto the headboard, to grip the wood rails, to brace herself for a hot, hammering ride.

Pushing her legs apart, he wedged between them, his eyes never leaving hers.

He lowered his head to nuzzle her breasts, to make

gumdrops out of her nipples. JJ drew a shaky breath and waited. Her heart was beating like a painted drum.

"Eight months," he whispered in her ear. "Of thinking about you, of letting you consume my mind."

And now she consumed his body.

He went after the condom. And then he went after her.

He thrust full hilt, nearly knocking the air right out of her lungs. She wasn't about to let go of the headboard.

He rocked her to the core, to the center of the earth. When he cupped her rear and lifted her off the bed, her hips slammed against his.

She could feel every power-driven stroke. In. Out. Deeper. Wetter.

He used his hand, slipping it between their bodies, rubbing her most sensitive spot, heightening the sensation, the blast of fire.

JJ shuddered in violent waves, and he watched her, focused—totally, completely—on her orgasm.

Lost, she wrapped her legs around him, the climax wracking her in two. She'd never been with a man who'd put her pleasure ahead of his.

She could feel the pressure building in his loins, the sexual insanity warring inside him. Yet he was holding back, waiting for her, wanting to be aware of every move she made.

Because of the obsession, she thought. Because he was memorizing her, absorbing her, taking her into his soul. The thought scared her senseless, but she could see it in his eyes.

Those dark, demanding eyes.

He kissed her, fierce and deep, and she released the headboard and bit her nails into his back.

And when he came, when he erupted like a hurricane, she prayed for mercy.

But it didn't work.

She fell deeper and deeper into the storm.

JJ didn't know how long Dylan stayed on top of her. Long enough to claim her, to hold her, to keep her as close as humanly possible.

"Am I too heavy?" he asked.

"No." She liked the weight of his body, more than she should.

He raised his head. "Are you sure?"

"Yes." She shifted her hips, felt him stir. He'd already ditched the condom, tossing it in the trashcan beside the bed, but he was still half-aroused. "Isn't that supposed to go away?"

"It is. It will." He breezed his mouth across hers. "But not if you keep moving around."

She smoothed a strand of hair away from his forehead, wished he wasn't so knock-down-drag-out gorgeous. "Then maybe you shouldn't kiss me."

"But I like how you taste." He cruised her lips again. "I like how we feel against each other, too. Hot. Sweaty."

"We had a pretty good workout."

"Yeah, we did. Do you want to take a shower with me?"

The invitation made her smile. No denying they needed one. "How about a bath instead?"

"In that big girly tub? You won't put any frou-frou stuff in the water, will you?"

She was still smiling. "I might."

He altered his weight, held her in place, kissed her. "You need to let a man keep his dignity."

She went warm, woozy. "And you need to let a girl keep her bath salts."

He grinned, scooped her up and hauled her into the bathroom. "Maybe smelling like you won't be so bad. I can sniff my own skin and turn myself on."

"Dylan." She looped her arms around his neck and let him charm her.

The big girly tub was white with sea-foam green tile and a mermaid décor. He set her down, and she turned on the faucet and let the water run.

When she dug through a container of bath salts, he leaned over her shoulder.

"This one is called water lily," she said.

He examined the cube in her hand. "Is that a clue?"

She turned to look at him. "For what?"

"The flower thing. You're driving me crazy with that." He pressed his body to hers. "Are lilies your favorite flower?"

She thought about the makeshift wedding bouquet

she'd held in front of the mirror as a child. She couldn't bear for Dylan to give her one just like it. And he would, she thought, if she gave him half the chance. "It isn't lilies. But this is my favorite bath salt."

"Then it'll have to do. For now," he added, taking the scented cube and dropping it into the water.

They climbed into the tub and sat across from each other. He leaned against the tile and drew his knees up. "This isn't so bad. It's actually pretty nice. Like the western days or something."

"When cowboys bathed in brothels? And saloon girls washed their backs?"

"Sort of, yeah." He laughed a little. "Of course I don't need a saloon girl, not when I've got you."

She wadded up a washcloth and flung it at him, hitting him square in the chest.

He stayed right where he was, with his head tipped back. The washcloth slid down his chest and plunked into the water. "I was kidding, Julia."

"You're always kidding." She splashed him, but he didn't budge. He was enjoying the attention.

And she was enjoying being so close to him. When he closed his eyes, she took the opportunity to study him. All those long, rangy muscles, all that sun-burnished skin.

He dropped his head back even farther, and she noticed the nasty scar way under his chin.

"What happened?" she asked.

He opened his eyes. "What?"

"Your scar."

He squinted at her, as if he couldn't fathom what she meant. And then he got it. "Oh, you mean this?" He tapped the area in question. "I busted it open when I was a kid. In the ring," he clarified. "I've been boxing since I was nine."

"Really?" She couldn't help her surprise. "You don't have a pugilist's face. You're too pretty for that."

"Pretty?" He shook his head, frowned. "What about guys like De La Hoya? And Sugar Ray?" He sat forward. "Not that I ever went pro. But I can hold my own."

She didn't doubt that he could. And now that she thought about it, she wasn't surprised that he used his fists on other men. Or that he'd gotten his chin split open as a kid. "I'll bet you were fighting with your peers first."

"I was. Between breakneck horse stunts and getting into schoolyard brawls, my parents were beside themselves. I wasn't like my older brother. I wasn't out to save the world. I was beating up on it." He made a meaningful expression. "It was my dad's idea to get me into Golden Gloves."

"Did it help?"

"For the most part, it did. I still blow off steam in the ring. When you were missing, I—"

"You what?" Her nerves tangled. "Beat the heck out of your opponents?"

He shrugged, swished the water. By now the water

lily bath salt had melted. "More like I let my opponents kick the crap out of me."

He confused her. "Why would you do something like that?"

"Nothing. Never mind. Just forget that I said it." He picked up the washcloth she'd tossed at him and wrung it out. "Let me wash your back."

She turned around, scowled to herself, wondered if he was keeping another secret.

And then he touched her, softly, gently, sponging soapy water over her skin.

Her mind went blank.

Her body went lax.

She sighed, and he put those strong arms around her, washing her breasts, her belly, the V between her thighs.

Making her fall under his possessive spell.

All over again.

Ten

Dylan woke up with his arm draped across Julia. To him, it felt like a perfectly natural way to start the day. Spooning or whatever it was called.

He nestled her hair. He was getting used to the pale color. With daybreak seeping into the room, the highlighted strands shimmered against the pillow.

She had sunrise hair, he thought. Warm. Airy.

Julia stirred, but she didn't waken. Dylan didn't mind. They were both naked with the covers bunched and tousled, and he liked the romantic disarray.

He could do this for the rest of his life. *Would* do this for the rest of his life, he amended. He'd meant what he said last night. Losing her wasn't an option.

Julia had accepted him for who and what he was. She'd forgiven him for his past, for all of that crap with Linda.

Everything was fine.

Yeah, right.

He still hadn't found a way to win Julia over completely, to forge a bond that couldn't be broken, to summon the strength to call the FBI, to tell Julia the truth about her mother.

He coiled his arm around her waist, holding her a little closer, a little tighter.

She arched her body, and he realized she was waking up, stretching like a curvaceous cat.

When she turned, they were eye to eye. With his secret between them.

"Hi." She greeted him with a Sleeping Beauty yawn. She had a roadmap, marks from the creases in her pillowcase, zigzagging the side of her face.

"Hi." He traced the lines and wished he could read the future in them, the way a gypsy read palms.

"Should I make coffee?" she asked. "Breakfast?"

He shook his head. "I'd rather stay in bed."

"Mmmm." She made a yummy sound. Sleeping Beauty was intrigued. She shifted her legs, maneuvering one knee across his.

He sucked in a breath, smiled, teased her, did his damnedest to temper the guilt, to stop worrying. "Are we playing Twister?"

She smiled, too. "That old party game?"

He glanced at the pattern on the quilt. "Your right foot is on the green swirl."

She went along with him. "And your left hand is on the yellow slash."

When he reached across her shoulder, going for a corner of white sheet, she grabbed him and pulled him down on top of her. He landed with a sexy thud and kissed her square on the mouth.

"I like this game," she said, after he came up for air.

He studied her. The roadmap was fading, but her freckles remained. Light, soft, barely there. Like sprinkles of salt. "Because you cheated."

"Listen to the man. You cheat all the time."

"Oh, yeah?" He used his weight, holding her down.

The teasing banter ended, and his nakedness branded hers. But that wasn't enough. He wanted to give her more.

As much as they both could endure.

He was slow, deliberate. He leaned forward to nuzzle her breasts, to take one of her nipples into his mouth, to use his tongue, the very edge of his teeth.

She wound her fingers into his hair, and he explored the budding hardness of her other nipple. Her heart vibrated, beating desperately, going as ragged as her breathing.

He moved lower, French kissing her stomach, making patterns around her navel, leaving marks of salvia on her skin. Her muscles jumped in anticipation.

He took his time, making her wait.

Her fingers tightened in his hair, and he slid down her body, all the way down, lifting her legs and bending her knees. But he didn't lower his head, not until he knew she was watching.

And then he did it. He made love to her with his mouth, swirling, tasting, drizzling moisture like honey.

She floated, she ebbed, she went taut with heat, with hunger. He could feel each and every warm, wicked, bordering-on-shy sensation.

When she came, she shuddered and shook, muffling the sensual sounds she made.

He'd never been so aroused.

He rose up to hold her and she clung to him, her breasts flattening against his chest, the area between her thighs damp and silky from his touch.

She didn't say anything, and neither did he. Without letting her go, without releasing her, Dylan reached for a condom and tore open the packet.

She helped him roll on the latex, their fingers brushing. He looked into her eyes, and she lifted her hips, giving him what he wanted, what he needed.

He drove himself upward, the contact searing his blood and making his head swim. His mind blurred, and he couldn't tell where his body faded and hers began. But it didn't matter. He couldn't think beyond thrusting inside her, beyond becoming one person, one entity.

They tumbled over the bed, and he spun her around, switching positions until she was straddling his lap, their bodies still locked good and tight.

The air whooshed out of her lungs, and she blinked, her lashes sweeping her cheeks.

He circled her waist and moved her up and down, setting the rhythm. She took over, riding him until they both shattered, until orgasms erupted like volcanoes.

She collapsed in his arms, and seconds turned into minutes. As their skin cooled, as sweat evaporated in the air, he worried about losing her again.

He got up, went to the bathroom, trashed the condom and splashed water onto his face, telling himself to get a grip.

But it didn't work.

He returned to bed and saw her sitting on the edge of it. "Can I borrow one of your shirts?" she asked, looking beautifully rumpled.

He nodded, and she rifled through the drawer where he'd unpacked his clothes, and slipped on a simple denim shirt, closing the western snaps and rolling up the too-long sleeves. The tails hung past her hips.

He grabbed a pair of jeans and zipped into them. She walked toward him, and he took her in his arms. She fitted her head against his shoulder, all snug and warm, steeped in the afterglow of soul-defying sex.

And that's when it hit him, when he figured out how to keep her, how to make her part of his everyday world, how to win her over, how to forge an ever-lasting bond.

"Marry me," he whispered in her ear, his voice deep and steady. "Become my wife."

* * *

Shock, confusion, panic.

Romantic amazement.

JJ couldn't begin to describe the emotions that grabbed her by the throat. That tugged at her heart. That had her stepping back and gaping at Dylan as if he'd gone cuckoo clock mad.

"Please tell me this is one of your jokes," she said, even though she knew it wasn't. She could see the seriousness in his eyes.

"I'm not kidding around," he told her. "I'm proposing to you. Here. Now."

"Why?" was all she could ask.

"So you'll stay with me. So we can live together. So we can be morally and legally bound."

"You're taking this too far." Nervous, she pillaged the pile of garments on the floor, the things he'd stripped off of her last night, and searched for her panties.

"I don't care," he said. "It's what I want. *You're* what I what."

She found her underwear and put them on. It was bad enough that she was wearing his shirt. That she needed to be impossibly close to him, even after he'd been inside her.

JJ took another step back, almost stumbled on the scatter of clothes. "Your possessiveness is taking over. The insanity you can't seem to stop."

He didn't revoke his proposal. Not one bit. Not one iota. "I just told you that I didn't care."

Logic didn't apply, she thought. Not to Dylan. And no to her. The little girl in the mirror, the child who'd secretly planned her wedding, wanted to accept his proposal.

Talk about insanity.

JJ was losing what was left of her mind. "I need to catch my breath. To get some air." She exited his room and headed for the bungalow's private courtyard, knowing Dylan would follow.

He wasn't about to leave her alone, not with his offer tipping the scales of their relationship, of their affair, of everything that was coiling up inside her and threatening to burst.

Once they were outside, she became aware of her surroundings: the dew on potted plants, a common-looking orange butterfly flitting in abandonment, birds singing morning songs, the wrought iron café table in the corner, the matching chairs with heart-shaped backs.

She inhaled, exhaled, took a moment to calm her nerves. Then she turned and looked at Dylan.

He stood tall and straight, his hands crammed in his pockets. Beard stubble peppered his jaw, almost too faint to see. The sun cracked through the sky, like a bright yellow ball fighting the L.A. smog and illuminating him in a strong, hard, marriage-minded glow.

"Say yes, Julia."

She shook her head. "No."

"We're good together. You know damn well we are."

Yes, they were good together. Too good. Too sexy. Too emotional. But he hadn't said anything about love, about the main ingredient that was supposed to make a marriage work.

It didn't matter, did it? Not unless she was falling in love with him.

And she wasn't, was she?

"I'll move to Nevada," he told her. "I'll buy some land near the refuge. I'll build us a house. Then you can stay close to Henry. You can—"

Overwhelmed, she interrupted him. By now her knees were getting weak. She didn't want to be in love with him. She didn't want to her heart to revolve around his. "You'd do that for me?"

"Yes."

The butterfly winged its way to another plant. "What about your horse farm? Your parents? Your life in Arizona?"

"I can relocate my horses and hire new ranch hands. And I can visit my parents. I can bring you home on holidays. And we can have kids. We can raise a family of our own."

The weakness got worse. She headed for the table and took a seat. Behind her, hanging ferns with delicate fronds grew in the shade.

"I thought you didn't want children," she said.

"I didn't. But only because I thought I'd be a

bachelor all of my life. But I want to settle down with you." He reached for one of the chairs, turned it around and straddled it, pressing against the heart design. "I wasn't conscious of it at the time, but I think what you said is true. When you disappeared, I relived the emptiness, the feeling that I lost something…someone…who belonged to me. The woman I'm supposed to marry," he added. "The woman who's supposed to bear my children."

He made her ache. Yet he still didn't speak of love. He didn't say what a man who is proposing should say.

"I fantasized about getting married when I was a little girl," she told him, needing to wash away the memory, to dispel it, to say it out loud and let it go. To stop herself from needing him, she thought, from hungering to be his wife. "I planned it in my mind."

"Really?" His eyes, filled with curiosity, with questions, locked onto hers. "How old were you?"

"About nine. About the same age you were when you got a crush on your brother's bride."

"I told Carrie about that." He squinted, pushed away the hair that trailed onto his forehead. "I didn't mention the bride part, but I told her I had a crush on her when I was a kid."

"What did she say?"

"Not much. She knew I was teasing her, flirting a little, trying to make her feel better. At the time, she and Thunder were having problems, and she was wary of marrying him again."

"You flirted with Carrie?"

"I told her that she could marry me instead of Thunder. But I was kidding. I wasn't the least bit serious."

"Did you make the same joking offer to Talia?"

"Yeah, I guess I did. Not long after they were married, I asked her if I stood a chance of stealing her away from my cousin. But I was just fishing to see if she was happy." He blew out a windy breath. "Aaron says I flirted with Talia at their wedding, too. They eloped to Las Vegas and I crashed the ceremony. Aaron was ticked about it, but I wanted to be there for Talia, to make sure Aaron was going to treat her right. They were getting married, but there was still a lot of pain between them, baggage from their past."

JJ couldn't help analyzing him. "For a man who expected to be a bachelor all of his life, you seem to have a thing for brides."

He shrugged, frowned, pushed a little harder into the iron-framed heart on his chair, practically transferring the design onto his bare skin.

"Tell me about your girlhood fantasy," he said, steering the conversation back to her. "About the wedding you planned."

She glanced toward the butterfly, but it was gone. "I didn't plan it in that much detail. Not the way an adult would have. But I got dressed up in front of the mirror."

He smiled a little. "In what?"

"A white nightgown of my mom's. It was frilly, all lacy and soft. And it had this flowing robe that that went with it. For my veil, I used a satin pillowcase, pinning it to my hair with shiny barrettes."

"I'll bet you looked beautiful."

His compliment made her uncomfortable. Because he meant it. She could tell how enraptured he was by her story. "I was trying to look like the bride in one of my old coloring books. In my mind, it was a fairy tale wedding."

"Who was the groom? Who did you envision at your side?"

She leaned back, struggled to breathe, felt a frond tickle her hair. "I don't know. He was a prince, I guess. Someone who would save me from—"

"From what?"

"Myself," she admitted. "I was a lonely child. Quiet. Withdrawn. Overly imaginative." She tried to laugh off her last comment, but her voice chipped instead, on the edge of crumbling.

"I could be him, Julia. I'm not a prince." He made a quick guarded expression. "Far from it." His shook away the tightness. "But I'll be a good husband. I'll give you everything. Everything I can."

Her pulse jangled. Like a church bell. A warning, she thought. An alarm. "I'm not ready for this."

"Yes, you are," he argued. "You've always wanted to be a bride."

"I was a child then. This is different. This is real." And so was he. Tall, dark, dangerous Dylan.

They sat quietly for what seemed like a long, lethal, drawn-out minute, tension snapping between them. She was glad she hadn't told him the rest of her story, about the bouquet she'd picked, about how significant those flowers were.

"I'm not accepting no for an answer," he said. "I can't. I won't. I'll keep trying. I'll keep asking you to marry me. To be the girl in the mirror."

He stood up, and she noticed that the chair *had* marked his skin. But not completely. The impression was only partially visible, branding him with half a heart.

The man determined to walk her down the aisle.

The man she was struggling not to love.

Eleven

It was good to be home, JJ thought. To be walking with Henry, to enjoy the mountainous backdrop, to be immersed in the refuge again.

She and Dylan had returned to the Rocking Horse two days ago, where they jumped headfirst into the final stages of the fundraiser.

Henry was thrilled with the money JJ and Dylan had raised in California. He was also excited about Dylan's clients, the Malibu partiers, who'd agreed to attend the actual event and bring their children, nannies and whoever else came with their cash-spending entourage.

Henry and JJ would be hosting a weekend fair, and

all the participants had agreed to donate either their time or a portion of their proceeds to the Rocking Horse. The fair included games, rides, concession stands, arts and crafts and farm animals. For entertainment, they'd gotten a western specialty act. And then, of course, there was Dylan. He would be conducting horsemanship demonstrations guaranteed to draw a crowd. For now he was in the barn, working with the horses that were up for adoption, leaving JJ and Henry to tend to other details.

But Henry's mind was elsewhere. "Dylan told me that he asked you to marry him."

JJ barely missed a loose stone beneath her foot. She hadn't been prepared to discuss Dylan's proposal with Henry. She was still trying to come to terms with it herself. "What did he say?"

"That he was willing to move here, to buy some acreage near the refuge. So you and I could remain close. So we could be like a family." Henry stopped walking. "He mentioned wanting to have babies with you, too."

"Well, then." JJ nerves bundled and bunched, like they'd been doing ever since Dylan came back into her life.

Henry nabbed her gaze, his pale blue eyes bursting with crow's feet, with lines depicting age and wisdom and too much sun. "Your kids would be like grandchildren to me."

She touched the side of his face, forced herself

to stay strong. "Dylan and I haven't even talked about love."

He gave her a baffled look. "Why not?"

She dropped her hand, unable to produce a logical answer. "We just haven't."

"That boy is heads over heels, and so are you."

"Are we?"

"Of course you are. You're worrying for nothing."

No, she wasn't. But she wasn't going to argue with her boss. It was clear that he wanted her to marry Dylan. That he saw himself and his long lost wife in their eyes.

"Did you know I have some of Dylan's training tapes?" he asked.

She shook her head. "I didn't even know he had training tapes." Which was foolish on her part. Dylan was well known throughout the country. Why wouldn't he have videos for sale?

"I ordered them from his web site. Long before he showed up here looking for you. Ironic, isn't it?" Henry went into idol worship mode. "Did you know he works with the Bureau of Land Management? Conducting training seminars featuring newly captured mustangs? We aren't the only adoption program he's affiliated with."

"I don't know much about his professional life." But she knew how it felt to lie in his arms, to kiss him, to attend diamond-draped parties where other guests watched them dance.

"He's good at what he does. Damn good. Handsome, too. You two would have some fine-looking babies."

"Henry."

"Can I help it if I'm itching to hold a little one on my knee?"

"You shouldn't try to persuade me like that."

"Why not? Because you can't stand to see yourself happy? Settled? Secure? You deserve to be free, JJ."

She frowned, shuffled her booted feet, shoved her hands in her jeans pockets. "Free from myself?" From the lonely child in the mirror, she thought, recalling what she'd told Dylan.

"I'll bet your mama would have liked Dylan. She's probably gazing down on you right now, wishing you'd accept his proposal."

"I'm sure you're right." Her eyes turned watery, burning from the memory of her mother's grave, from kneeling on the grass beside Dylan, from the tender things he'd told her about the burial.

Henry touched her shoulder, squeezing lightly, his arthritic fingers bent. "Don't give up a good thing."

"I'm not ready. I'm just not—"

"Why? Because you don't want to admit that you love him?" He shook his head, pursed his lips, let out a paternal tsk. "In my day, young folks weren't afraid of the American dream. Finding someone to love, getting married and raising a family was what we strived for."

"What I feel for Dylan is complicated."

"Then you ought to tell him. Explain what's going on inside you."

"Maybe I will." And maybe she wouldn't. Her emotions were too jumbled to make clear-cut decisions.

Henry gestured to the barn, a building that had been freshly painted, bright and pretty for the fundraiser. "Why don't you go see him, honey? Watch him work. Get to know a little more about him."

JJ took Henry's suggestion and wandered into the barn by herself. Although she kept her distance, she located Dylan with a horse named Clay, a sorrel gelding that had suffered from neglect.

Dylan glanced up and spotted her, and when their eyes met, her heart jumped, rushing forward to play tag with his.

They hadn't been sleeping in the same bed. Henry had put Dylan up in the guest room. Hopeless romantic or not, Henry lived by old-fashioned rules, preferring that unwed couples remain celibate under his roof. What they did away from his house was their business.

At the moment, Henry's rule seemed like a good excuse to marry her lover. JJ missed him desperately.

Dylan didn't break contact with the horse. He appeared to be desensitizing Clay, gentling the high-strung gelding, getting him used to his touch.

JJ moved a little closer. Clay didn't react. He didn't shoot her a spooked look or jerk his head like he normally did. Dylan's method was working.

She stood for the longest time just watching them, man and horse, forming a bond. No wonder Henry admired Dylan. Within a day, he'd established a relationship with Clay, a gelding she and Henry struggled to reach.

Finally she turned and left them alone. When Dylan was ready, he would come and find her.

And probably ask her to marry him all over again.

Dylan came to her an hour later. JJ told herself she wasn't waiting for him, but she knew better.

He walked forward, then stopped in front of her. She was sitting on the ground beside an ancient pine tree with a massive trunk and contorted limbs.

She looked up at him. She had a spiral notebook on her lap with a fundraiser to-do checklist. "This is my favorite spot on the refuge."

"I can see why. That tree is amazing."

"It's dead," she said, and made him frown.

He sat in the dirt beside her, getting his already-dusty Wrangler's a little dustier. "It does look kind of haunted."

"This species can survive for thousands of years, even after it dies." She wanted to touch him, to kiss him, but she fussed with the notebook instead.

"Maybe we should carve our initials on it. Then we'll survive for thousands of years, too." He leaned forward, reached out to smooth a wayward strand of her hair. "I'm going stir crazy without you."

"Me, too. But we can't—"

"I know. Henry has his rules. I won't disrespect him." Dylan tucked the misbehaving hair behind her ear. "At least we'll be going back to California right after the fundraiser."

She tilted her head. "We will? What for?"

"My brother's wedding. I figured we could stay at the same hotel. Get our old bungalow."

And relive the sex, she thought. Make love until they were spent, until the bed spun in vertiginous circles.

"After Thunder's wedding, we can plan our own." He took her hand in his. "Say you'll marry me, Julia."

His expression, his gut-wrenching intensity, pierced her like one of the jagged branches on the tree.

"I'm afraid of loving you," she said out loud.

He started, jerked back a little.

She'd caught him off guard. She'd knocked herself off kilter, too. She hadn't meant to blurt it out. Not like that.

Silence. Complete silence.

She fidgeted with the notebook again, uncoiling the top edge of the wire. "I'm sorry. I shouldn't…"

"It's okay. I haven't even—"

"Considered being in love?"

"Isn't being obsessed with you enough?" He clenched his fist and made a mock gesture to his stomach, as if he were punching himself. "It hurts. Like a bruise that won't heal."

Her fear magnified, and she uncoiled the wire a

little more, leaving a sharp piece exposed, lacerating the paper. "Maybe we should just leave things be."

"Leave them be? Not if that means you won't marry me. I can't wake up every day without you."

"I need more time. I need—"

He cut off her off with a kiss, his mouth pummeling hers, like the bruise inside of him, like the confusion inside of her.

Lost, she wound her arms around his neck. He tasted like the breeze, like the late spring air, like the snow that had already melted in the mountains.

Cool. Fresh. High-elevation deep.

When they separated, she wanted to crawl all over him, to rip open his shirt, to claw his heart, to let herself fall desperately in love.

But a mortal danger held her back. Because something wasn't right. Something she couldn't explain. A premonition of sorts. The darkness she kept seeing in his eyes.

"How long are you going to make me wait for an answer?" he asked.

"I don't know." She wondered if they *should* carve their initials in the dead tree, it would make them stronger.

"I'll wait for the rest of my life," he said, following her gaze to the lone pine. "Thousands of years if that's what it takes. I'll never want anyone but you."

"You're making it worse, Dylan. You're making me more afraid."

"I can't help it." His dug his nails into the dirt. "I can't help the way I feel."

And neither could she. JJ was trapped in the turmoil he'd created, in a would-be vow that made her ache.

"I have to go back to work." She opened the notebook and showed him her to-do list, her hands much too shaky. "If I don't, I'll never get everything done before the fundraiser."

"Kiss me one more time," he said.

"Then what? You'll let me get back to work?" Her frustration peaked. "You don't own me."

"Yes, I do. The same way you own me. We're in this too deep to get out."

She didn't want to agree with him. She didn't want to make herself more vulnerable than she already was. But it was too late for that.

"One kiss," she whispered, hating herself for needing him so badly, for letting him mess with her emotions.

Their lips met softly, gently, and then she summoned the power to pull back, to stand up and walk away.

Organized chaos, Dylan thought. On the day before the fundraiser the carnival equipment: game tents, inflatable activities, concession stands and rides were being erected, expanded or built. From his vantage point, he could see an air castle and a moon bounce. In the distance a Ferris wheel turned in a test run.

Determined to keep his mind occupied and his

muscles active, Dylan helped Henry's ranch hands build animal pens for a local 4-H club competition. One spry little kid had been hanging out half the day, making sure the containment for his pig met his satisfaction.

Billy or Bobby or whatever his name was looked up at Dylan, unaware, or unconcerned, about how busy the men were. "Did you know that pigs like to be pampered?" he asked.

Curious, Dylan crouched down. Kids normally didn't pay him any mind. "No, I can't say that I did."

"Well, they do. They like to have their ears and bellies rubbed. And they like apples for treats."

Billy or Bobby was a fair skinned boy with a messy flop of dark blonde hair and a cowlick that would have made Dennis the Menace proud. He looked about eight, maybe nine. The magic age, Dylan thought.

"I've been getting ready for this show for weeks," the child said, puffing up his chest and looking much too proud.

Strangely charmed, Dylan smiled. "I'll bet you'll win a ribbon."

"I'll bet I will, too. I washed and clipped Louie, and I'll clean him up again before I take him into the ring."

"Louie? That's your pig's name?"

"Uh, huh. I named him after my grandpa. My mom's dad."

Dylan chuckled. Behind him, a few of the ranch hands laughed, too. They were eavesdropping on the conversation. "Did that make your grandpa happy?"

"He doesn't know about Louie. Grandpa died last year." The boy made a face. "He was my only grandpa. The only one I had left."

No more laughs. No more chuckles. "I'm sorry," Dylan said. "Both of my grandfathers are gone, too. I never met my dad's dad. He died before I was born. But I was close to my mom's dad before he passed away."

"Would you have named a pig after him?"

"I don't have any pigs. I've got horses, though." Dylan was still crouched down, eye level with Billy or Bobby, wishing he would have paid attention to the kid's name.

Then he imagined choosing names for his own children. He'd been thinking about raising a family since he'd asked Julia to be his wife. Thinking long and hard about it.

But that didn't mean he wanted to dwell on love, to define it, to make himself any more obsessed than he already was.

Dylan got to his feet. How much more could he ache? Could he want her? Could he need her?

He glanced at the inflatable castle, wondering if it reminded Julia of her childhood, of the fairy tale she'd manifested, of the prince Dylan could never be.

He was okay with Julia being afraid, as long as she accepted his proposal. What was wrong with living happily-ever-*fearful*-after? As long as they were together?

He turned and saw her coming toward him. All

long and lean and pretty. And frazzled. By the time she got closer, he knew something was wrong.

He searched her gaze, but she avoided the question in his eyes. He wondered if the fundraiser was becoming too much for her, if one of the rides were faulty or if some of the food that was scheduled to arrive had spoiled on a damaged refrigeration truck.

"Barry," she said to the boy. "Your mom is ready to go. She's at the house with Henry."

"Okay." The kid grinned up at Dylan. "I'll see you at the fair, mister."

"Sure." Barry, he added mentally. Not Billy or Bobby. He'd gotten the boy's name totally wrong.

After the kid was gone, Julia looked right at Dylan. He moved away from the ranch hands, and she followed him, creating a disturbingly private moment.

"What happened?" he asked, reaching out to soothe her.

She pulled back, refusing to let him touch her. "You left your cell phone at the house."

Praying that his heart didn't hit the fan, he struggled to steady his emotions. "And?"

"It rang, and I answered it. I should have let your voice mail get it, but I…" She paused, removed his phone from her pocket and extended the now-silent device. "It was the FBI. Special Agent McLaughlin."

He took his cell, opened the case, snapped it shut, wished he could break it. "Did you tell McLaughlin who you were?"

"Yes, I did. And he was shocked. He had no idea that you'd found me." Her lips thinned. "You lied. You told me that you'd talked to the FBI. That they knew I was with you."

"I'm sorry. But I had my reasons."

"Did you?"

"Yes." He tried not to panic, but his stomach was threatening to cramp. Could he salvage this? Could he fix it? Weave another lie to get past it? "Did McLaughlin tell you why he was calling me?"

"To talk to you about your testimony."

Everything inside him went still. "Did he say anything else?"

"He said I should ask you about your testimony, then call him back to confirm the truth."

Dylan flinched. "The truth?"

"To make sure you give me the whole story. That you don't leave anything out. He isn't sure if I should trust you." Her voice broke, shook, nearly shattered. "And neither am I."

Twelve

Dylan's world crashed in on him. But there was nothing he could do to stop it.

"I didn't want to lose you," he said.

"So you kept me in the dark?" She gazed at him, wariness in her eyes. "Why? What's in your testimony?"

He stalled for a moment, looking past Julia and gazing at the fair in progress. The Ferris wheel was still turning in a test run, and so was the carousal. Colorful ponies moved up and down, the brass-ring music resounding in the late spring air.

She snapped at him. "Tell me, Dylan."

Feeling like a zombie, he turned his attention back to her. "It was my fault."

"What was? What are you talking about?"

"Your mother's murder."

Julia's skin went pale, her barely-there freckles more pronounced. She didn't respond, but he could tell that she didn't know what to say. That she was locking her knees, trying to stay strong, waiting for him to expound.

He continued, blowing out a breath. By now, his lungs were clenched. "After you and your mother ran away, I started poking around in your lives and figured out that your mother owed money to loan sharks."

"How does that make you responsible for her murder?"

"I went to the authorities, and they agreed that the loan sharks had motive to kidnap you. But there was no evidence linking them to the crime. So I—"

"You what?" Her voice broke, like it did earlier.

"I threatened the loan sharks. I told them I was going to find you and bring you and Miriam back to testify. A few weeks later, I got an anonymous tip that a hit man had been hired to kill both of you. To stop you from testifying."

"And now it's a murder trial," she said.

"But it shouldn't have been. The kidnappers wouldn't have a hired a hit man if I hadn't forced their hand. They don't normally kill people for owing them money. They threaten them, they scare them, but they don't shoot them."

"Because they can't squeeze money out of a corpse?" Her eyes turned red, watery. "Did you ever find out who gave you that tip? Who warned you? Who was trying to protect my mother and me?"

"The FBI didn't know at the time, but now they think it was a man named Steven Carter. He was part of the loan shark's organization, but he wanted out. He wanted to get away from them."

"Did he?"

"No. The hit man shot him, too." Dylan glanced at the Ferris wheel. It was no longer turning. The carousal was still, too. "Thunder was with Steven when he died. They'd arranged a meeting, and when Thunder got there, Steven was lying in a pool of blood. My brother tried to save him, but he couldn't."

"I wish Thunder had been there for my mom. That he'd tried save her. That she hadn't died alone."

Suddenly Dylan felt as if he were dying, as if Miriam were reaching for him, pulling him into her grave. "I'm sorry. I'm so sorry."

"For what? My mother's murder?" Tears hit her cheeks. "It's your betrayal that hurts. The secrets. The lies."

Dylan didn't respond, and a pounding hammer echoed, along with the buzz of an electric drill. The ranch hands were still building animals pens.

"When did you hire Thunder and Aaron to look for me?" she asked, gathering facts, pushing him for more information.

"After I got the tip about the hit man. After I knew I'd screwed up."

"Does your family know that you lied to me?"

"No. But I would have told you. I would have come clean."

Her gaze challenged his. "When?"

"After we got married. After you—"

"Oh, God." She gripped her stomach. "That's why you proposed to me? To alleviate your guilt?"

"No. *No,*" he argued. "I proposed to you because I was afraid of losing you over this. Because you're everything to me. Because I can't shake you from my blood."

"You can't shake your guilt. That's what you can't shake." More tears came, more emotion, more pain. "You're confused about why you want me, why you think you need me."

"That isn't true." He longed to hold her, to bring her warm and tight against his body, to ease her sorrow, her suffering. But he just stood there, drenched in his own anguish. "I wanted you before Miriam died. I wanted you from the moment I first saw you."

"And this is our fate? Our destiny? You lying to me? Keeping me from the FBI?"

"I wouldn't have kept you from the trial. I wouldn't have let it go that far. I was just trying to buy some time." He paused. "I didn't know what else to do."

"I can't handle this." She fought another crying jag. "I just can't."

"I'm sorry." He apologized again. "I never meant to hurt you."

"But you did," she said, stepping back, putting even more distance between them. "You did."

When she walked away, he let her go.

Praying that it wouldn't be forever.

The fundraiser was in full swing, and JJ was a mess. She roamed the event with frazzled nerves and sunglasses to hide her swollen eyes. She'd cried half the night.

This was going to be the longest weekend of her life.

The refuge was packed, bustling with activity, with people enjoying the day, eating junk food, drinking sodas, playing games and going on rides. Dylan's Malibu clients had arrived, and by tomorrow they would be bidding on the horses that were up for adoption.

JJ stopped to view a row of brightly colored tents, showcasing prizes waiting to be won. She approached the shooting gallery, then glanced at a ring toss game.

She hadn't spoken to Dylan since yesterday. Because every time she saw him, her eyes welled up.

"JJ?" a graveled voice called out to her.

She turned, knowing it was Henry. He was walking around, too. Playing host. Talking to his guests.

He moved closer and they gazed at each other. She adjusted her dark glasses, making sure they were firmly in place and grateful that it was a sunny day.

Of course she wasn't fooling Henry. He'd seen her this morning over breakfast, over a quick bowl of instant oatmeal, with her eyes unmasked and her tears threatening to fall. Dylan had skipped breakfast. He'd gone straight to the barn to groom the horses.

"How are you holding up?" her boss asked.

"I'm okay. I'm—"

"Still hurting over Dylan?"

She nodded, swallowed the lump blocking her throat.

"What Dylan did was wrong, honey. Lying to you like that. But his heart was in the right place."

"He's obsessed with me, and he's guilty about my mother. But that isn't a reason to marry me."

"What about you?" The older man frowned. Behind him, a little girl squealed when her daddy won a stuffed bear and gave it to her. "Have you admitted that you love him?"

She didn't answer. Because she didn't want to think about it. Not now. Not while she was at the fundraiser.

A local rancher approached Henry, and his conversation with JJ was cut short. Relieved, she wandered away, giving her boss a shaky wave, letting him know she was disappearing into the fair.

But no matter how hard she tried, she couldn't escape. The sights and sounds magnified, closing in on her. The popcorn aroma got stronger and just walking past a ride called the Ghost Train made her shiver.

How much grief could she bear? Wasn't the loss of her mother enough? Did she have to fall apart over Dylan, too?

Unable to stay completely away from him, she headed for his demonstration, where a crowd gathered. Instead of weaving her way to the front, she lagged behind the other spectators so he couldn't see her, so their eyes couldn't meet.

He was on horseback, wearing an earpiece microphone, looking every bit the professional horseman he was. He wasn't letting his emotions show.

Attired in varying shades of denim, with his hat dipped low and his hair falling to his shoulders, he demonstrated a training technique designed to build trust between horse and human.

And the paradox made her eyes well up again.

What about trust between a man and a woman? Between lovers? Dylan hadn't built that bond. He'd left JJ floundering.

She slipped away before his demonstration ended, forcing herself to get through the fundraiser, to do her job, to help save the Rocking Horse Refuge.

Even if she couldn't save herself. Even if she knew that she loved him.

On Sunday night after the fundraiser ended, JJ answered a knock on her bedroom door. There stood Dylan, with a bouquet of her favorite flowers.

How did he know? When had he figured it out? Or was this a coincidence? A romantic accident?

"Can I come in?" he asked.

She nodded, allowing him access to her room, trying to rein her emotions, trying to keep her heart from slipping.

The tiny blooms were blue with yellow centers, clustered together to maximize their delicate beauty and long, spindly stems.

The only place to sit was on her bed, so she didn't offer him a seat. They both remained standing.

He extended the bouquet. "They're forget-me-nots."

She took the floral arrangement, avoiding her reflection in the closet mirror.

"I asked the florist what I should give to the woman I'd just lost," he said. "And she suggested forget-me-nots. So you would never forget me." He winced a little. "You don't think that's corny, do you?"

"No, not at all." She struggled to steady her breath. She wanted wrap her arms around him, to cry against his shoulder, to mourn the pain between them. "I know all about forget-me-nots."

"You do?" He searched her expression. "Is this them? Are these your favorite flower?"

"Yes," she responded, memories tripping like a hopscotch stumble. "When I was young, our neighbor used to grow them. She planted them from seeds, and I watched them bloom every spring."

"Did she tell you about the medieval legend?"

JJ nodded, recounted the story. "A knight and a lady were walking along the side of the river. He knelt to pick her some flowers, but his armor was so heavy, he fell into the river. While he was drowning, he tossed the flowers to the lady and asked her to 'Forget-me-not.'"

"I feel as if I'm drowning," Dylan said.

So did she. As if someone was holding her head under water.

"Did you call Agent McLaughlin?" he asked suddenly. "Did you confirm the truth?"

"Yes, I did. And he apologized for telling me that I shouldn't trust you, for making a personal issue out of your testimony. But he's still angry that you kept me away from the bureau."

"McLaughlin is the agent who cut through the red tape so I could take possession of Miriam's body, so I could bury her. I guess he feels betrayed now, too."

"He doesn't blame you for her murder. He said that if you hadn't put pressure on the loan sharks, the FBI would have."

"Yeah, but they would have handled it differently. They wouldn't have put you or your mother in danger." Dylan looked as if he wanted to stalk the room, but there was nowhere to go. The wall-to-wall furniture, the bed, the oversize dresser, the twin night-stands, had him trapped. "The assassin should have come after me instead. I should have been his target."

"Oh, God. Don't say that." She reached out to

console him and dropped the bouquet. The forget-me-nots spilled onto the hardwood floor, scattering like tiny blue weeds, their leaves and stems akimbo.

JJ knelt to pick them up, to scoop them back together. Dylan descended to help her, and their gazes met over the debauched flowers.

She tried to salvage the moment, to make it less tragic. "Remember when I told you that I dressed up in front of the mirror?"

"As a bride? Of course I do."

She smoothed a crumpled petal, a bent stem. "I was holding a bouquet of these."

"Damn. Really?"

She explained further. "Sometimes forget-me-nots are used in wedding bouquets. They're associated with happily-ever-after." With faithfulness, she thought, and enduring love.

"The florist didn't tell me that. But maybe she was hoping they'd bring us luck."

Luck? She recovered the flowers and both she and Dylan came to their feet.

She waited for him to tell her that he loved her. But he didn't. Silence stretched like the dead of time.

"I'm leaving tomorrow," he said, reminding her that he'd purchased two tickets to California. "I wish you were coming with me."

"I can't. Not now. Not after everything that's happened."

He removed her ticket from his pocket and set it

on the dresser. "I'll leave this anyway. Just in case you change your mind and want to take a later flight. The wedding isn't until Friday, but I have to be there a few days early. To attend the rehearsal and pick up my tux and all that." He placed JJ's invitation on the dresser, too. "I'm a groomsman or an usher or whatever it's called."

She didn't respond. She didn't want to picture him in wedding attire. But he didn't give her a choice.

"Instead of flowers, the men are wearing crystal boutonnieres." He glanced at the forget-me-nots. "If we were getting married, I'd be wearing one of these."

She blinked back tears, and he reached out to touch her.

"I'll wait for you. For the rest of my life," he said, repeating what he'd told her on the afternoon they'd sat beneath the ancient pine tree. "If you want me, I'll always be yours. But I won't come back, not unless you ask me to."

He wasn't giving up, she thought. But he wasn't saying that he loved her, either. The words continued to escape him.

She ached to kiss him goodbye, to feel his mouth against hers just one more time. But she knew it would only make things worse. So she stepped back, making sure it didn't happen.

He left her room, and the next day he was gone.

Thirteen

The chapel sat on a hill, overlooking the ocean.

Originally Carrie and Thunder were going to get married on the beach in broad daylight, but they'd decided on a church wedding instead, choosing an evening ceremony.

Dylan arrived early, suited up and ready to go. He'd been too anxious to stay at the hotel by himself.

He glanced at his watch, frowned, and sat on the wooden steps of the chapel, with stained glass windows and a steeple behind him. For now, the building was closed.

He was the only person here.

Talia and Carrie were the next to arrive. But they

weren't dressed for the occasion. Together they unloaded makeup cases, crystal-and-seashell bouquets and garment bags from the car.

Dylan approached them, and Carrie glanced up at him.

"What are you doing here?" she asked. "The wedding isn't until seven. Did you get the time mixed up?"

"I know when you're getting married."

"You meant to be this early?"

"Yes."

Carrie exchanged a girly look with Talia, and he suspected that they wanted to comfort him. But he wasn't about to expose his emotions.

"I was bored at the hotel," he said. "Do you want some help with that stuff?"

"Sure." Carrie gave him a sister-in-law smile, and he took the clear-plastic garment bag from her hand.

"I'll be careful," he told her. He knew it was her wedding dress. He could see white lace and crystal beads.

He followed the women to a dressing room on the side of the chapel. Talia, the matron of honor, unlocked the door with a key that must have been provided. They went inside, and Dylan glanced around.

"So this is where the bridal party gets ready?" The question was redundant, but he was out of his element. The room was frilly with lots of mirrors and an attached bathroom.

"This is it," Carrie responded.

Before things got even more awkward, he placed her wedding gown on a closet rod and stepped back. "I should go. Let you ladies do your thing." He paused, turned to Carrie. "I'm glad you're marrying my brother again."

She reached out to hug him. "So am I."

Afterward, he looked at Talia, and she embraced him, too.

"Aaron is lucky to have you," he whispered. Six years ago Talia had been left in the dust when Aaron had married someone else instead of her. But eventually he'd found his way back to Talia—the woman he truly loved.

"JJ is lucky to have you, too," she whispered back, aware that he'd arrived early to wait for Julia, to hope that she came to him.

"Thanks." Uncomfortable, he released his cousin's wife and exited the bridal room.

Dylan spent the next few hours wandering the chapel grounds and studying the ocean below. The hilltop view didn't put him at ease, but he did the best he could.

He didn't want to ruin his brother's wedding.

When Thunder and Aaron arrived, Dylan congratulated the groom, a man he'd admired—and envied—for most of his life. He wasn't about to admit how he felt, but he suspected that somewhere deep down Thunder knew.

They gazed at each other in a silent yet poignant exchange.

Then Aaron spoke, "Here we are again," he said, as they gathered in front of the chapel, dressed in matching tuxes. Aaron had been the best man last time, too. "Twenty years later."

Thunder smiled. "Yeah, but Dylan was only nine then. Look at my kid brother now."

Oh sure, he thought. Look at me now. Waiting for a woman who might not come.

The woman he loved.

The revelation hit him like a ton of soul-crumbling bricks.

Yet there was nothing he could do. He'd left himself wide open, trapped at her mercy, hundreds of miles away.

He'd promised to wait for her, to let the choice be hers. But now he wanted to return to Nevada and storm the refuge instead. To forgo his promise. To force her to spend eternity with him.

But he couldn't.

Soon the guests began to arrive, and Dylan and the other groomsmen ushered them inside. Dylan's parents and Carrie's mother were seated in front, and Carrie's dad waited to walk his daughter down the aisle.

Julia didn't arrive with the other guests, but Dylan tried not to give up hope.

To lose heart.

He watched Carrie and Thunder repeat vows in a

candlelit ceremony, but he kept looking for Julia, praying that she would slip quietly into the chapel.

Only she never did.

JJ clutched her invitation, bending the corners of the silver-scrolled paper and entered the banquet room, where the Trueno-Lipton reception was being held.

Guests gathered at linen-covered tables or swayed on the dance floor. A lavender and blue color scheme shimmered throughout the room, and ornately draped windows and circular-shaped balconies provided oceanfront views.

She stood back and searched for Dylan, but she didn't see him. There were too many people, too much activity. She caught sight of the bride and groom and watched them dance among the crowd.

Thunder wore a traditional black tux, and Carrie's crystal-beaded gown showed off her baby bump. Her loose, full hair, embellished with silver ribbon and seashell ornaments, caught the light.

The meal had been served, but the cake hadn't been cut. JJ noticed the three-tiered desert, in all its frosted and sugared finery, on a lace-clothed table.

Finally she inched forward and saw Dylan. He was on the dance floor. At first she couldn't tell who his partner was, but then she realized it was his mother.

Margaret Trueno gazed at her youngest son while they moved to a classic Sinatra song.

Dylan looked dark and brooding, the way he often

did. JJ wasn't the only woman in the room watching him. A group of attractive twentysomethings had their eye on the groom's sexy brother.

Someone bumped JJ's arm, and she moved out of the way for two children, a tuxedoed boy and a lavender-gowned girl, who grinned up at her and darted off to stand by the DJ.

She assumed the kids were part of the wedding party. Just like Dylan. She returned her attention to him, and the song ended.

Dylan escorted his mother back to their table, glanced up and saw JJ from across the room.

Her heart nearly stopped.

He shook his head, as if his mind were playing tricks on him, as if JJ were a mirage.

Then he started toward her, passing the young women who'd been ogling him. But he didn't seem to notice.

JJ didn't even try to meet him halfway. Her legs were too rubbery to move. Now that she was here, her fear intensified.

Was she doing the right thing?

While Dylan weaved his way though the other guests, the DJ announced an Elvis song.

By the time Dylan reached JJ, *Love Me Tender* sounded softly through the speakers.

"I waited for you at the church," he said, his eyes fastened on hers. "And when you didn't show, I..."

"Didn't think I was coming?" She couldn't stop

looking at him, either. "I wasn't sure if I should. But I took a last-minute flight."

He reached out to touch her sleeve, to finger the imitation silk. "You're wearing my grandmother's dress."

"I wore it for you. For your family." She paused, wished she wasn't so nervous. "I couldn't stay away. I tried to forget you, but I couldn't."

"Forget-me-not," he responded roughly, as Elvis's song drifted between them.

Like flowers blowing desperately in the wind.

"I love you," JJ finally managed. "That's why I came. To tell you how I feel."

His held her gaze, held it like a vise. "And wait to see what I would say? To base your decision on my response?"

She nodded. "As much as I want you, I can't stay with you if you don't feel the same way."

"But I do," he told her. "I swear I do."

"Since when?" she asked, the floor nearly shifting beneath her feet.

"Since forever, but I just figured it out today." Dylan knew he couldn't hold back. But he didn't want to. He wanted to tell her everything he'd been contemplating for the past few hours.

And Julia was ready to hear it. He could feel her expectation mounting.

"I know it sounds crazy, but I've loved you from the first moment I saw you," he said.

She angled her head, as if she were considering

him, trying to make sense of his admission. "You didn't even know me."

"I knew that I needed you. That you changed something inside me. But I told myself it was fate, destiny, obsession. I wasn't supposed to be the kind of guy to get caught up in clichés. Love at first sight. Me? The serial bachelor? No way."

She reached for his hand. "Did your denial escalate after you found out about the hit man?"

He squeezed her hand. "Totally. And it got worse after your mother died. I wasn't about to admit how I felt, to acknowledge what was happening. Not even after you told me that you were scared of loving me."

Her smile was shaky. "I'm not anymore."

He smiled, too. Even if his heart was clamoring its way to his throat. "You still look a little scared."

She leaned against him. "So do you."

He gathered her in his arms and held her as close as he possibly could. Everything about her was familiar. The way she fit against his body, the scent of her skin, the texture of her hair.

"I'll call you JJ if you want me to," he said. Because it didn't matter what name she preferred. She was, and always would be, the woman he loved.

"I'd rather be Julia to you."

He rubbed his cheek against her hair. "Will you marry me?"

"Yes," she responded, without the slightest hesitation. "I want to share my life with you, to have your children." She looked up at him. "I think it's what my mom would have wanted for me, too."

"I'll always be sorry that you lost her. That I was part of that loss."

"I know you will. And that makes me love you even more. You're a good man. An honorable man."

He kissed her, and everything but the two of them disappeared. Their lips met soft and sweet and pure.

Later that night after Dylan's family welcomed Julia, after everyone celebrated his brother's wedding, Dylan took Julia to the hotel room he'd rented.

The same bungalow as before.

With the lights burning low, she moved closer, unpinning his boutonniere and placing it on the nightstand.

"I should have caught the bouquet," she said.

"It doesn't matter." Because she'd already agreed to marry him, to be his bride.

"You're right." She loosened his tie, and he wondered what kind of ring he should buy her, what kind of diamond she would want.

His jacket came next, then his shirt. Bare-chested, he folded her into arms, and her abalone necklace, the one he'd given her, scraped his skin. But he liked the primal sensation.

"You're mine," he said. "You're really mine."

"Always," she told him.

She finished undressing him, and he did the same

thing to her, discarding her dress, unhooking her bra, removing her panties.

Naked, they climbed into bed, the sheets cool and inviting. Her hair tangled across the pillow, and he tipped her chin and kissed her.

His woman. His world.

Igniting the foreplay, he ran his hands over her body, up and down, caressing her curves. She touched him, too, arousing him, creating shivers.

And when she wrapped her legs around him, he penetrated her hard and deep, letting the feeling, the being-in-love passion, carry him away.

Epilogue

Sunlight danced in the air, streaming in from a second-story window, and blue balloons and brightly colored flowers decorated the hospital room.

JJ sat in bed, watching her husband cradle their one-day-old son.

Dylan glanced up and smiled. "I love you, Julia."

She couldn't imagine a more beautiful moment, even after twenty-two hours of labor and the C-section that had followed. Her body ached in places she couldn't begin to describe. "I love you, too."

"Look at our boy." He stood and walked over to the bed, keeping the baby close to his chest. "Isn't he amazing?"

"He's the most perfect child on earth." She reached out to touch the cap of dark hair that crowned the infant's head. "Matthew Curtis Trueno."

They'd chosen Matthew because it meant gift of the Lord, and Curtis because it was Dylan's middle name, as well.

"He's such a stubborn little guy," Dylan said, as the blanket slipped and the baby pushed his fists through the opening.

JJ nodded. She knew how sweetly stubborn he was. After all of those hours of labor, she'd had a C-section because Matthew refused to move down the birth canal. He'd wanted to stay in her womb.

Suddenly the door opened and Henry entered the room. The older man moved forward, his gaze lighting on JJ, then on Dylan and the baby. This wasn't his first visit. He couldn't get enough of Matthew.

Henry was their neighbor, their friend and the baby's surrogate grandpa. True to his word, Dylan had built a house near the refuge, allowing JJ and Henry to remain close. Along with Dylan, they kept the Rocking Horse alive, hosting fundraisers and horse adoptions.

Dylan handed Matthew over to Henry, letting him enjoy the infant's waving fists.

"What a kid," Henry said, proud as a feather-bursting peacock.

Soon the room filled up with more visitors, with everyone Dylan and JJ loved. Thunder and Carrie arrived with Tracy, their toddler in tow. Tracy, with her ruffled dress and bow-shaped barrettes, behaved like a spry little angel in her daddy's arms.

Aaron and Talia brought Danny, Aaron's bright-spirited son from his first marriage. Although Aaron and Talia had waited awhile, they'd finally decided that the time was right. They were in the stages of planning a baby of their own, hoping to give seven-year-old Danny a brother or sister.

Not that there weren't enough Trueno offspring to go around. Carrie was pregnant again, and she and Thunder were eagerly awaiting their second child, another daughter, according to a recent ultra sound.

By the time Dylan's parents arrived to beam over Matthew, the Trueno clan was complete.

Later that night when the room was dim and quiet, JJ nursed her son, holding him gently against her breast.

Dylan sat in a nearby chair, watching her and listening to Matthew suckle. JJ knew that Dylan would always be there, protecting her and their child until his dying day.

He really was her prince, she thought. The man she'd dreamed about all of her life.

The man who'd rescued her heart.

* * * * *

A special treat for you from Harlequin Blaze!

Turn the page for a sneak preview of
DECADENT
by
New York Times *bestselling author*
Suzanne Forster

Available November 2006,
wherever series books are sold.

Harlequin Blaze—Your ultimate destination
for red-hot reads.
With six titles every month, you'll never guess
what you'll discover under the covers...

RUN, ALLY! Don't be fooled by him. He's evil. Don't let him touch you!

But as the forbidding figure came through the mists toward her, Ally knew she couldn't run. His features burned with dark malevolence, and his physical domination of everything around him seemed to hold her like a net.

She'd heard the tales. She knew all about the Wolverton legend and the ghost that haunted The Willows, an elegant old mansion lost by Micha Wolverton nearly a hundred years ago. According to folklore, the estate was stolen from the Wolvertons, and Micha was killed, trying to reclaim it. His dying vow was to be reunited with the spirit of his beloved wife, who'd taken her life for reasons no one would speak of, except in whispers. But Ally had never put much stock in the fantasy. She didn't believe in ghosts.

Until now—

She still didn't understand what was happening. The figure had materialized out of the mist that lay thick on the damp cemetery soil. A cool breeze and silvery moonlight had played against the ancient stone of the crypts surrounding her, until they joined the mist, causing his body to thicken and solidify right before her eyes. That was when she realized she'd seen this man before. Or thought she had, at least.

His face was familiar…so familiar, yet she couldn't put it together. Not with him looming so near. She stepped back as he approached.

"Don't be afraid," he said. His voice wasn't what she expected. It didn't sound as if it were coming from beyond the grave. It was deep and sensual. Commanding.

"Who are you?" she managed.

"You should know. You summoned me."

"No, I didn't." She had no idea what he was talking about. Two minutes ago, she'd been crouching behind a moss-covered crypt, spying on the mansion that had once been The Willows, but was now Club Casablanca. And then this—

If he was Micah, he might be angry that she was

trespassing on his property. "I'll go," she said. "I won't come back. I promise."

"You're not going anywhere."

Words snagged in her throat. "Wh-why not? What do you want?"

"If I wanted something, Ally, I'd take it. This is about need."

His words resonated as he moved within inches of her. She tried to back away, but her feet were useless. "And you need something from me?"

"Good guess." His tone burned with irony. "I need lips, soft and surrendered, a body limp with desire."

"My lips, my bod—?"

"Only yours."

"Why? Why me?" This couldn't be Micha. He didn't want any woman but Rose. He'd died trying to get back to her.

"Because you want that, too," he said.

Wanted what? A ghost of her own? She'd always found the legend impossibly romantic, but how could he have known that? How could he know anything about her? Besides, she'd sworn off inappropriate men, and what could be more inappropriate than a ghost? She shook her head again, still not willing to admit the truth. But her heart wouldn't play along. It clattered inside her chest. The mere thought of his kiss, his touch, terrified her. This wildness, it was fear, wasn't it?

When his fingertips touched her cheek, she

flinched, expecting his flesh to be cold, lifeless. It was anything but that. His skin was smooth and hot, gentle, yet demanding. And while his dark brown eyes were filled with mystery and wonder, there was a sensitivity about them that threatened to disarm her if she looked too deeply.

"These lips are mine," he said, as if stating a universal fact that she was helpless to avoid. In truth, it was just that. She couldn't stop him.

And she didn't want to.

* * * * *

Find out how the story unfolds in...
DECADENT
by
New York Times *bestselling author*
Suzanne Forster.
On sale November 2006.

Harlequin Blaze—Your ultimate destination
for red-hot reads.
With six titles every month, you'll never guess
what you'll discover under the covers...

REQUEST YOUR FREE BOOKS!

2 FREE NOVELS PLUS 2 FREE GIFTS!

Passionate, Powerful, Provocative!

nocturne™

HER BLOOD WAS POISON TO HIM...

MICHELE HAUF

FROM THE DARK

Michael is a man with a secret. He's a vampire
struggling to fight the darkness of his nature.
It looks like a losing battle—until he meets
Jane, the only woman who can understand his
conflicted nature. And the only woman who can
destroy him—through love.

On sale November 2006.

SAVE UP TO $30! SIGN UP TODAY!

INSIDE *Romance*

The complete guide to your favorite
Harlequin®, Silhouette® and Love Inspired® books.

✓ Newsletter ABSOLUTELY FREE! No purchase necessary.

✓ Valuable coupons for future purchases of Harlequin,
  Silhouette and Love Inspired books in every issue!

✓ Special excerpts & previews in each issue. Learn about all
  the hottest titles before they arrive in stores.

✓ No hassle—mailed directly to your door!

✓ Comes complete with a handy shopping checklist
  so you won't miss out on any titles.

- -

SIGN ME UP TO RECEIVE INSIDE ROMANCE ABSOLUTELY FREE

(Please print clearly)

_____

Name

_____

Address

_____

City/Town   State/Province   Zip/Postal Code

Please mail this form to:

(098 KKM EJL9)   **In the U.S.A.:** Inside Romance, P.O. Box 9057, Buffalo, NY 14269-9057
In Canada: Inside Romance, P.O. Box 622, Fort Erie, ON L2A 5X3
<u>OR</u> visit http://www.eHarlequin.com/insideromance

IRNBPA06R   ® and ™ are trademarks owned and used by the trademark owner and/or its licensee.

Silhouette
Desire

COMING NEXT MONTH

#1759 THE EXPECTANT EXECUTIVE—Kathie DeNosky
The Elliotts
An Elliott heiress's unexpected pregnancy is the subject of high-society gossip. Wait till the baby's father finds out!

#1760 THE SUBSTITUTE MILLIONAIRE—Susan Mallery
The Million Dollar Catch
What is a billionaire to do when he discovers the woman he's been hiding his true identity from is carrying his child?

#1761 BEDDED *THEN* WED—Heidi Betts
Marrying his neighbor's daughter is supposed to be merely a business transaction…until he finds himself falling for his convenient wife.

#1762 SCANDALS FROM THE THIRD BRIDE—Sara Orwig
The Wealthy Ransomes
Bought by the highest bidder, a bachelorette has no recourse but to spend the evening with the man who once left her at the altar.

#1763 THE PREGNANCY NEGOTIATION—Kristi Gold
She is desperate to get pregnant. And her playboy neighbor is just the right man for the job.

#1764 HOLIDAY CONFESSIONS—
Anne Marie Winston
True love may be blind…but can it withstand the lies between them?